THE GIRL AND THE FIELD OF BONES

A.J. RIVERS

PROLOGUE

SECONDS AFTER DEATH.

The dead have thoughts.

In the seconds after death, as all oxygen leaves the brain, a surge of activity fires every neuron-like one last bolt of lightning. Every path lights up. Every connection, every potential thought, makes one final rush to the surface. No one knows what those thoughts are.

The dead can't speak.

But they can remember.

For those final seconds, they are more alive than when they took their first breath. The brain churns out thought, grasping for anything and everything. This will be the last.

By the time her face splashed into the dirty puddle in the cracked asphalt, her brain was flashing with every moment she had ever lived. Every breath. Every voice she ever heard. Every word she ever said. It was all there.

And just as quickly as it passed, it was over. Her head lolled in the hands that lifted it up from the puddle. She didn't feel her feet being dragged across the pavement or the loose gravel tearing holes in her pantyhose.

TWENTY MINUTES AFTER DEATH.

The dead can bleed.

The heart has stopped, but for several minutes, blood continues to flow through the veins. By force. By memory. By sheer inertia. But then it stops. There is no more heartbeat, no more pressure. The blood stops, the capillaries empty, and the color of life drains away. Soon the blood will pool where it stopped, darkening to red and purple and black. But for a time, all is pale.

She was nearly translucent by the time the trunk closed over her. If she was still breathing, her lungs would have dragged the smell of cotton and heat into her lungs. Lips losing their moisture stuck to the cloth, but her eyes were closed. They couldn't have seen the dark.

THREE HOURS AFTER DEATH.

The dead hold tight.

What takes months to build and grow takes only a fraction of that time to break down. But the body doesn't give up gently. It rages against death. It holds onto every shred of life. Within hours, as the brain lies dormant and the heart drains fully of blood, the muscles clench and tighten. The entire body goes stiff, holding the position it assumed upon death. It will stay that way for a couple of days before relinquishing itself to finality.

It was hours after the trunk closed over her that she was given over to the ground. She didn't know it was cold and wet, more mud than dirt. But the hands that dug down into it knew. It wasn't easy to get her into the trunk. It was harder to drag her curled, hardened body to the hastily dug grave. Harder still to dig around her, to force away more of the mud and tangled roots, so she would fit.

She could have ended up anywhere, yet somehow this felt like the only option. It was the only place that made sense. Here she wouldn't be alone. Even if no one ever knew where she was. And that was the plan. No one would ever know. She would just fade away, be forgotten.

But it was beautiful here. At least there was that.

That soothed some of the guilt.

The rest of the guilt was buried with her. Soaking through the cloth with raindrops. It stayed with her as the mud came down, and the earth swallowed her. It would cover her as time continued to pass.

Five days after death.
Two weeks after death.
Six months after death.
Ten years after death.

TWENTY YEARS AFTER DEATH.

The dead tell secrets.

CHAPTER ONE

"Dead?" Dean asks. "What do you mean he's supposed to be dead?"

"Exactly what I said," I tell him, walking around the side of the car. "Darren Blackwell, better known as the Dragon. Major drug lord. Organized crime. He had airtight control over his massive syndicate. The Bureau had him under investigation for years. They wanted to close the case by sending somebody undercover. I was new and unknown. So, they chose me."

"What happened?" Dean asks.

"A story for another time," I say. "But the last I heard of him was that he was dead, buried in a prisoners' field. Nobody claimed his body."

"If he's dead, why would Lydia Walsh have notes about him for her little cold case website? And why would the members of Prometheus react to his name?" Dean points out.

"I don't know. But it wouldn't be the first time in my life somebody came back from the dead," I note.

I climb in the car, and Dean gets in behind the wheel. We drive back up the uneven dirt road to the temple. What was a pocket of deep darkness earlier is now flashing in blue, red, and white. Different patterns and tempos to match the vehicles parked haphazardly on the grass.

"Why did they send a rescue squad?" Dean frowns as we pull up beside Sam's car and climb out.

"Standard procedure," I say. "Any time they think there might be conflict, they like to have emergency response vehicles handy. Just in case."

I meet his eyes, not needing to put out into the universe the words going through my mind. Various officers move in and out of the building. I jog up to the doorway and step inside.

There is a distinctly different feeling in the building now. It's hard to explain. It doesn't feel lighter, as if some sort of exorcism had occurred to cleanse it once the members of The Order of Prometheus left under cover of darkness. Instead, it's hollow. Like a shell. There should be something in here, and even though it isn't here now, the impression still lingers. It's the same feeling I get when walking through an old crime scene. There's energy in the air, an indelible mark on the atmosphere itself that I can feel around me.

"Emma," Detective Noah White calls over, coming toward me. "Good to see you in one piece."

"I don't suggest you make that your usual greeting," I comment. "But thanks for the sentiment. Are you sure everyone is gone?"

He nods. "The crew swarmed the place as soon as we got here and checked every room we had access to. We didn't find a single person."

"The rooms you have access to?" I ask. "What do you mean?"

"Most of the doors in the building are locked. We were only able to get into a few of them, and they were pretty much empty," he explains.

"Locked? That doesn't make any sense."

"They weren't locked when you were here?"

"No," I say.

Sam comes up behind me. His hand rests on my lower back like he's trying to steady me.

"What is it?" he asks.

"The doors are locked," I tell him. "They weren't locked when Dean and I were here. We didn't try many of them, but there was an office and the sanctuary. Were you able to see either one of those?"

"No," the detective says.

Sam shakes his head in agreement. "I haven't been able to see much of it, obviously, but from what I hear from the guys who've been here, they're not seeing anything that you described. Not that it isn't in here, just that the doors are locked, and they can't get through them."

"So, open the doors," I shrug.

Noah shakes his head. "You know as well as I do we can't do that. We can't go into any of the rooms that are locked or blocked. We don't have probable cause or reason to believe a crime is currently being committed. The word of an FBI agent who was in the act of breaking and entering when she saw those things doesn't work as cause."

"So, you just—won't do anything?" I practically sputter. "There was a group of men in ceremonial robes ten seconds away from murdering me and tossing me out into a cornfield. The same men who are responsible for Lakyn Monroe's death, as well as the deaths of however many people are out in that field where she was. Not to mention Andrew Eagan, whose death means Xavier Renton is still sitting in prison for something he didn't do."

"Emma, I understand you're upset. I am too. If there was something I could do right now, I would. But you know that I can't. I need you to think clearly on this right now and understand that we have to follow procedures."

I know we do, but it doesn't make it any easier. I hate standing here in the building where Dean and I were not an hour ago and feeling as if the answers have just slipped through my fingers.

"So, what now?" I sigh.

"We'll keep the building under surveillance," Noah tells me. "I'll make sure it's constantly watched, so if anybody tries to go inside, we'll see him."

"How about the men? Sterling Jennings. Lorenzo Tarasco. Mason Goldman, also known as Eleanor Goldman. The warden. Are you going to keep track of them if they show up?" I ask.

"Emma," Sam says. "We can't put surveillance on them. You know that. Even if we wanted to bend the rules a bit, these are all well-known and respected members of the community. No jury in the whole county will take our word over theirs. If we want to take these guys down, it's got to be an absolutely iron-clad case. We can't afford to cut any corners. And as of right now, they aren't technically under suspicion for anything. We can't just harass them. We have to wait."

"Or get a warrant," I reply. "If we can get a warrant for the temple, we'll be able to open any door we want."

"We can try," Noah says. "I'll see what I can do."

The next day, I walk into the hotel room and kick off my shoes mid-step. Without slowing down, I walk into the bathroom and turn the faucet on full blast. Pressing the heels of my hands into the counter, I lean over the sink and take a deep breath. I fill my hands with water and splash it into my face a couple of times.

"How did it go?" Sam asks, coming to the door of the bathroom.

I snatch one of the hand towels off the metal bar attached to the wall beside the sink and press it against my face as I walk past him back into the main portion of the hotel room. Tossing the towel onto the bed, I start to undress. I just want to be in something comfortable right now.

"He's still there," I say.

"I know," Sam says.

I look into his eyes, shaking my head. "He's still there, Sam."

"I know," he repeats, his lips pulled tight in sadness.

"He didn't do anything. We know who murdered Andrew Eagan and why, and yet Xavier is still sitting there in that screwed-up facility under the thumb of those awful cultists. He still has people tell him when to get up in the morning and when to go to bed at night. When he can eat. If he's allowed to go outside his cell."

"He won't be in there forever," Sam says.

"He can't be," I say. "They have to give him a new trial. With a new judge. They need to let him out."

"What did he say when you told him what happened?"

I let out a sigh and go to the dresser for a pair of stretch pants and an oversized long-sleeve t-shirt.

"He told me the apple on a tree doesn't mind the time it takes to ripen. Makes for a better apple pie."

"What does that mean?" he asks.

"That he's been waiting this long already. He can keep waiting," I say. "But I'm not willing to let him keep waiting. Not if there's anything I can do about it. I promised him I would do everything I can to get him out of that place and get him a new trial as fast as possible."

"And when he does get his new trial?" Sam asks. "The lawyer has to prove there is sufficient new evidence to even start the trial. But after that, he has to create an effective enough case to convince people the courts got it wrong the first time. That's not something that happens too often. How is he going to prove he wasn't involved in Andrew's death and that it was actually Lorenzo Tarasco who did it?"

"That's what we have to figure out next," I say.

CHAPTER TWO

EIGHT WEEKS LATER ...

Another bone comes up from the dirt. It wasn't buried. Not formally, anyway. From the way it was positioned and the grass and weeds growing around it, it looks as if this is one of the bones that was just scattered throughout the cornfield.

Thinking about it makes my skin crawl. Not because I have a problem with the bones. But because I have a problem with the way they were treated. These were once people. They aren't props or ancient remnants. No more than a handful of years ago, they were living, breathing human beings.

Until someone took them and tossed them out among the rows of corn to be forgotten. Now I know the real benefit of the cage that was put over Lakyn Monroe's body.

It wasn't put over her while she was still alive. That had been my first thought when I first saw it. I thought someone had caged her and left her out to die of exposure and starvation. But the cage was too lightweight, too weak to hold a human being inside. It was put in place after she was already dead. And after weeks of watching the forensics team collect and unearth bones and remnants of who these people once were, I understand why the cage was there.

It protected her. It kept the animals away and stopped them from tearing her apart and scattering her throughout the field the way the others were. For many of them, parts of their bodies will never be found. They've been taken far away and will never be seen again. It's entirely possible there will be people who we will never be able to identify because too much of them has gone missing.

We may not even know how many are here.

But we know who she was. We found all of her—at least, what was left—because of that cage. I don't understand how it came to be there. I described it to Xavier, but he didn't have an explanation for me. Not even one that I couldn't understand. According to him, she should have just been discarded the way all the others were. But someone had a different idea.

And because she knew her minutes were numbered, she used the very last grains of sand counting of her life to leave a message detailing where she was going. Her final gift was making sure we knew where to look for her. And because of the cage, we found her.

And because of her, we found the others.

And we keep finding them. It's been two months now, and the excavation is still going on. It hasn't been continuous. Autumn storms and red tape have slowed progress. It's infuriating. Every day that goes by, I watch more people come up from the field and have to keep waiting. I know who did this. And there's nothing I can do.

"Explain to me again why we haven't been able to get back into the temple, Detective," I tell Noah, as he wipes dirt from his forehead with the back of his arm.

"Because we haven't gotten a warrant, Emma. You know that. We have to have a search warrant in order to go inside and open any of those doors. Right now, there is no clear-cut evidence that anybody who is inside that temple did anything wrong. Unless you want to get technical and count you and your cousin for breaking in," he replies.

"How are we supposed to get a warrant? You know who's involved in all this. The judge, the warden, some of the most powerful people in Harlan are wrapped up in The Order of Prometheus. How are we supposed to get a search warrant to prove they are responsible for what's looking like more than a dozen deaths so far? And that doesn't even include the ones involved in the initiation rituals."

"Emma, you know this. You have to think clearly about it. You have to remember that the law works in a specific way. Just because it doesn't always fit perfectly with what's going on, and just because it's not always fair or convenient, doesn't mean we can just toss it away and make our own rules," he says.

"Clearly, you don't know Emma Griffin very well," Sam comments, walking past with another plastic tray filled with bits of evidence.

He has spent the last month traveling back and forth between Harlan and Sherwood so he can keep up with his responsibilities as Sheriff while also continuing to help with the investigation here. It feels like most of the time we've been able to spend together has been out in this cornfield or running around from place to place in town trying to get somebody to listen to us.

But he's here. That means everything.

"We have to be able to give them a good reason," Noah protests. "There has to be probable cause that would give us a reasonable need to go in there. Just saying that you know what's going on and you saw suspicious things while you were illegally accessing the building isn't enough. Anything you saw is inadmissible as evidence. We'd be wasting our time and effort going that route without clear-cut evidence."

"What about everything that Xavier has told us?" I ask. "He's being held for a crime he didn't commit, and the people that are supposed to be watching over him used his heart condition to manipulate his state of mind so that he would be less trustworthy. But he has still been able to give us specific and reliable bits of information that have proven true every single time."

"If you can understand them," Noah points out.

"I can!" I say. "At least, most of the time. And now that he's being more closely monitored and hasn't been getting the huge doses of sugar to trigger his anxiety and panic attacks, he's much easier to understand. It's because of him that we even knew what the temple was, or to look for the black spheres. What he's given us and what I found should be more than enough to grant him a new trial. Finding Lakyn Monroe alone should be enough."

"Her death didn't have anything to do with Andrew Eagan's murder. Xavier has been in prison for that murder for years. The two don't look connected," he says.

"How can you possibly say that?" I ask, following the detectives as we head over to a large yellow plastic container of water set at the edge of the section of cornfield being excavated today. "She was working with him on that very case; she had gone into the temple and taken pictures of all of the evidence and was investigating it for him then she was murdered."

"I know what it looks like. And I know what happened. But until we're able to get a warrant, we can't go into that temple. We can't collect any evidence. The pictures that she took, the pictures that you took, your eyewitness testimony. None of it matters if we can't nail these guys, Emma. This has to be done the right way. I'm sorry."

Noah walks around me and goes back to the section of the grid that has been formed over the cornfield. It's the only way to organize a search of this magnitude. The sprawling space has been cut into smaller pieces and strategically placed posts hold ropes that bisect each of the rows, creating neat little squares. Each of them is thoroughly searched for any sign of a body's having been there, or for the remnants of one that have found its way to that spot.

Technicians collect dirt samples to analyze for body fluids that have sunk down into the dirt. Bits of bone, fabric, teeth, broken electronics, jewelry. They are all carefully sifted out of the dirt and collected into plastic trays that are photographed and recorded. It's all that's left of those lives.

A car door slams a few yards away. My jaw sets, and my hands briefly curl into fists at my sides when I see him. Long, determined strides bring me across the ground until I am steps away from Creagan.

"Why haven't you interceded?" It's all I can do to keep from shouting at him.

"Good morning, Griffin," he starts. "Nice to see the sun out after so many days of rain, isn't it?"

"Those days of rain have made mud, that is now covering the people digging bodies out of the cornfield. Enough bones to make at least fourteen people. And I know who did it. I can't do shit about it because I can't get back into that temple. Nobody will get me a warrant. So why haven't you done anything about it?" I demand.

"We have to tread lightly on this one, Griffin," Creagan says.

"Don't give me that," I snap. "The Bureau got involved in this because I fed you the information about Lakyn Monroe. You wanted in on it, and now I am. So, do something about it. You can supersede the authority of the local judges and get us into that temple."

"And if I storm in there demanding to be given full access without justifiable cause, it's just going to make drama. It could potentially taint the investigation. We have to be careful. You need to stay calm and steady on this one. We'll figure it out. But we have to be patient."

CHAPTER THREE

TWENTY YEARS AFTER DEATH ...

The weight of the dirt lifted off her bit by bit.

After so long, it had compressed down from the first loose shovelfuls that landed over her into a thick layer encasing her. The raindrops that fell as the ground closed around her had long since sunken down through her and into the earth below.

They had become part of the groundwater. They brought a little of her into the streams. They evaporated back up in the summer sun and rained back down. Countless times. Over and over. Raindrops fell and seeped down through the dirt, through the cotton fabric, through her. They washed into the river, flowed through the streets. Became drinking water, filled bathtubs, streamed through sprinklers that cast rainbows, water dancing on children's skin.

Bit by bit, the weight lifted.

There were voices around her now. Cries of shock and surprise. Questions. There would be so many more of those. Those first bits of sunlight in twenty years touching the sheet that only told the very beginning of all her secrets.

It took several sets of hands to lift her out. The sheet sagged with the weight of water and mud and what was left of her inside. They tried to do it with dignity. They tried to offer her some respect as they brought her up out of the darkness and into an afternoon so much warmer than the last one she ever felt.

Placing the sheet down carefully on a blue tarp spread across the ground, they took pictures and spoke in hushed tones. It seemed as if they were buying time. For now, it was just a wet, deteriorating sheet. Once white and crisp, now dingy and fraying. It was just a sheet. Even if they could feel the drag of what was inside pulling it down. Even if they could see the discoloration on the fabric where the years and the raindrops melted her away.

Finally, there were no more pictures to take. They couldn't hesitate any longer. Gloved hands carefully unwrapped the layers to reveal her bones.

Fabric still clung to them. Bits of a long jacket and outdated dress. A necklace hung from her spine and tangled with her collarbone.

More pictures, measurements, and notes. Carefully moving each bone would reveal a ring long ago released from a finger as it lost its flesh.

"Any ID?" one of the voices asked.

"No," another responded. "No ID, no wallet, no phone. Nothing."

"So, who is she?"

CHAPTER FOUR

"Hey, Emma," the nurse at the station waves as I walk out of the elevator.

"Hey, Gloria," I smile. "How are you doing this afternoon?"

"Good," she says. "Fall allergies are starting to get to me."

"Well," I say, "it's a good thing you work in a hospital. Just raid the drug cabinet."

She laughs. "I think that's one of those perks, isn't it? It's listed in my benefits package as a bonus."

"Exactly," I say. "How is she today? Is she awake?"

"She's up," Gloria tells me. "She seems to be recovering really well. The infection is gone, and the doctors say they can see the light at the end of the tunnel."

"That's great," I tell her. "I'm going to go back and see her, okay?"

"Sure. You know where to find her," she says.

I flash the round, redheaded nurse a grin and head down the hallway to the last room on the left. It's the one with the best window on the floor. I made sure of that. Rapping my knuckles on the partially open door, it edges the rest of the way open, and I step inside.

"Hello?" I whisper in.

"Emma?" Millie answers, pushing herself to sit up a little higher on the reclined back of the hospital bed.

"Hey," I say. "I'm not interrupting anything, am I? You're not training for a marathon or getting ready for a grand ball, or anything, right?"

She laughs. "Nope, just finished with my thirty-mile run for the day. My glam team is supposed to show up in a couple of hours, but the red carpet can wait for a visit from you."

I settle into the chair beside her bed. It's hard to see her like this so long after the shooting. But when the bullet tore through her chest, it caused extensive damage, and she's had to undergo several surgeries over the last month-and-a-half. There have been a few times when the doctors weren't sure they would be able to keep her here.

But she has turned the corner and is looking stronger. There's more color in her cheeks, and she seems to have more energy.

"How are you feeling today? Gloria tells me things are going pretty well," I say.

Millie nods. "The last surgery was a success. I've gotten rid of the infection, and the doctors think I'm really on my way to recovery now. I might actually be able to get out of here in a couple of weeks."

"That would be great," I tell her. "I'm sure you're looking forward to not being in a hospital bed."

"Definitely," she says. "Not necessarily looking forward to going back to my house and seeing what that aftermath is like. A couple of months with no one inside probably isn't too kind to things like the food left in my refrigerator."

"Don't worry about that," I say. "I'll make sure it's ready for you before you go home."

"You don't have to do that, Emma," she protests. "You've already done so much for me."

"Again, don't worry about it. You can't go through this alone. So, I'm here to be your not-alone person," I say.

"And I really appreciate it. I just wish I could help you."

I shift around in my seat a little. Moving a little closer, I put one hand on the bed beside her.

"I think you can, Millie," I say. "I know you said you don't remember anything you said to me..."

"I don't," she says. "I'm sorry. Everything the day I got shot is a blur. All I remember is getting up in the morning and going into work. The next thing I knew, I was waking up here after my first surgery. I don't remember anything else."

"Nothing? You don't remember anything?"

"I'm sorry, Emma. I wish I did," she says. "I keep thinking about it and trying to remember, but I just can't."

"We were in the parking lot," I tell her, going into the same story I've gone over with her probably a hundred times since she's been in the hospital. "I was walking across the parking lot to my car, and you came out of the bank. You said you needed to talk to me about something. You needed to tell me something about your brother. You looked as if it was really serious. Then the car came up, and you were shot. Before you passed out, you told me to stop your brother. That I should look at the alibis."

She shakes her head. "None of that sounds familiar. I don't remember any of it."

"But can you remember what you wanted to tell me? Or think of something you might want to say? Because I did exactly what you said. I looked at all the alibis, and that's what helped me figure out what happened. I know about The Order, Millie. I know about the temple and the wheel. I know about the elder members sponsoring new members with an initiation that involves... murder. But I think you know more," I say.

Some of the color that gave me so much hope when I first came into the room disappears. Her eyes are a little wider, a sheer veil of tears over them. She shakes her head. I'm about to ask another question when the door opens again, and someone comes into the room.

I turn to look over my shoulder and feel my jaw tighten and my eyes narrow.

It's Lydia Walsh. She nearly stomped all over our investigation, but that's not the reason I'm mad at her. I'm mad at her because she randomly showed up at my ex-boyfriend Greg's hospital bed, discharged him somehow, and less than an hour later, he wound up dead. And she still has the nerve to proclaim her innocence.

"What are you doing here?" I ask.

"I'm here to see Millie," she protests. The liar.

"You have no reason to be here," I say. "You need to go."

"I don't think that's your decision, Agent Griffin," Lydia shoots back. "If you can come here to visit her, then I can, too."

"I know exactly why you're here," I snap. "And you need to stop."

"What's going on in here?" Gloria asks, coming into the room and looking between Lydia and me with her eyebrows knitted together and a concerned expression in her eyes. "We don't need shouting on this floor. People are trying to recuperate."

"I'm sorry," I say. "Lydia, can you step outside and speak with me for a minute?"

"Sure," Lydia replies coolly.

I look over at Millie. "I'll be right back."

Millie nods, swallowing hard. Gloria fills her a glass of ice water and brings it over to her with a straw, standing by her side while she sips it. I feel guilty for upsetting her, but I can't just ignore what happened the day she was shot. As she walked across that parking lot, she told me she needed to talk to me about her brother. Only seconds later, the bullets tore through her, and she collapsed into my arms. While I tried to stop the bleeding, she told me to stop him.

She knows something. It's in there. I just have to help her find it. And get her to tell me.

"What. Are. You. Doing. Here?" I ask Lydia in a low, hissing whisper when we get out into the hallway.

"I'm visiting Millie and making sure she's alright," Lydia responds.

Her eyes flicker back in the direction of the door, and the muscles through my body tense up. In my mind, I can see her checking on Greg the same way. I still don't know exactly what happened the day he was discharged from the hospital and left with her. All I know is that he was supposed to wait there for me or another member of the team, and instead, he walked out with her. The surveillance footage showing him walking across the parking lot with her is the last image of him alive I ever saw.

He was dead mere hours later.

"You don't even know her," I say. "You never even spoke to her before she was shot."

Lydia seems to think about this for a few seconds, then her shoulders drop, and she lets out a sigh.

"I just want to help, Emma," she says.

"Help with what?"

"The investigation."

"You are not a part of this investigation, Lydia. You need to stop interfering," I say.

"I'm not interfering. I want to be a part of it. I think I could be a valuable asset. I do know a few things about digging into cold cases," she says. "And I've already found out a few interesting things. Did you know Lilith Duprey, the woman who lives behind the cornfield where the bodies were found, hasn't always lived in Harlan?"

"Yes, I did know that. I found that out when we found out that she owns the house in Salt Valley, where Mason Goldman has been living."

"Right. But she also hasn't always lived in Salt Valley. As a matter of fact, she has never lived this far away from a city. She wasn't exactly a nature girl in her younger days."

I blink, almost incredulous at what this woman is trying to tell me.

"So?" I ask.

"So, why would a woman who has always lived in cities and is used to the finer things in life suddenly decide to settle in the middle of nowhere?"

I take a step closer to her. "Lydia, stop. This is serious. It's not a game. You need to back off and let the real investigators handle this before you hurt the investigation."

"Fine," she says, holding up her hands in a show of surrender and stepping back from me. "I just thought I could help. I'll leave."

"Thank you," I say, turning back toward Millie's room.

"Oh," she adds, making me turn around. "I meant to ask you. What was the key for?"

"What key?" I ask.

"The key Greg gave me to give to you."

CHAPTER FIVE

Those words stop me still. It takes a second before I'm able to really process them and respond.

"Which key? Why did Greg give to you to give to me? I don't know what you're talking about. You never gave me a key," I say.

"That's because I don't have it anymore," Lydia says.

"What do you mean you don't have it anymore?" I ask, stepping toward her again. "Where is it?"

"I gave it to the police when I talked to them about Greg's death," she says.

"Why the hell would you give it to the police?" I demand, my voice creeping higher again.

Lydia recoils slightly from my reaction. "He gave it to me the day he left the hospital. I told you we had made plans to get together, but he said there was something he had to do first. He gave me the key and said just in case, to make sure you got it. I didn't know how to get it to you, then when the police questioned me, I told them about it. They asked me for it, and I gave it to them. I figured they would make sure you got it because you were working with them."

"I wasn't working with *them*," I say angrily. "I was working with the FBI. The local police department didn't do shit about his murder and

25

still haven't. How could you just let him hand you a key like that and walk away? He said he wanted you to give it to me 'just in case'. That means he thought something was going to happen."

Lydia shrugs and takes a slight step back from me. "I thought he might be going to do something that had to do with his disappearance or an investigation, but I didn't ask. I figured if he wanted me to know, he would tell me."

"And when he was found dead that very night? You didn't bother to get in touch with anybody? You didn't call the police or try to find a way to contact me? You knew something must have happened, and you didn't do anything about it."

I'm raging at her at this point. Gloria's image of peaceful convalescence be damned. I'm so pissed I can't see straight, and I need Lydia out of my sight.

"I'm sorry. I didn't want to interfere," she stammers.

"Then you need to take your own advice now. Get out," I growl.

"Emma, I—"

"Get out!" I repeat angrily. "You need to stay away from me and everybody else involved in any of these investigations. You've already caused enough damage."

She turns and rushes away. Gloria pokes her head out of the door and gives me a disapproving look.

"Emma," she says. "Please."

"Gloria, I'm sorry, but I have to go. Tell Millie I'll come back and see her soon and to let me know if she needs anything."

She nods, and I jog to the elevator, in the opposite direction of where Lydia had made her way to the stairs. I'm already on the phone with Creagan by the time I cross the parking lot to my car.

"Did the DC police give you a key?" I rush out the instant he answers.

"Hell—a key?" he asks. "What are you talking about?"

"Back in DC. Did the police give you a key? I just talked to Lydia Walsh. She told me that Greg gave her a key to give to me the day he died. She gave it over to the police when they interviewed her. I know you knew they interviewed her, so do you have the key?"

I have no more patience left for this man. But his position in the Bureau means that as long as I am just an agent, I answer to him. He provides access to resources and privileges I don't have at my level. Which means I just have to deal with his bull and work around him as much as I can.

"Griffin, I don't know what you're talking about. I haven't heard anything about a key," Creagan says. "Where are you?"

"I'm just leaving the Harlan hospital. I'm going back to my hotel," I say. "I'll talk to you later. Call me if you find out anything new."

Before he can respond, I hang up and get in my car. Taking a quick glance into the backseat, I toss my phone and purse onto the passenger seat and pull out of the lot, headed to my hotel room. Once inside, I call the detective who was in charge of what amounted to the Police Department investigation into Greg's disappearance and murder nearly three years ago.

"A key?" he asks. "I don't think I remember a key."

"Think really hard," I tell him, struggling to control the tone of my voice.

"Actually, now that you mention it, I do remember that blonde woman coming in to talk to us. You had seemed so interested in finding out why she was with Mr. Bailey, but she didn't really have any information to share that seemed to mean anything," the detective says.

"I'm well aware that you dropped the ball on the chain of information," I say. "That's not why I'm calling you. I talked to Lydia Walsh today, and she told me that she gave you a key when she went in for her interview. It was intended for me."

"That's right," he says. "She said he gave it to her before they parted ways that day. That it was supposed to go to you just in case."

"So why didn't it?" I asked.

"She gave it over to us," he says. "I guess it got put aside somewhere, and nobody thought to give it to you. I'm sorry about that."

I cringe and wish I could remember one of those mantras my therapist taught me back when I was ordered to attend regular sessions with her. She told me they would calm me down and help me maintain control. This would be a fantastic time for me to put that to the test.

"What happened to it?" I ask, my hand clamped so tight over my temples I feel like I'm about to pop.

"If it wasn't in the evidence passed over to the Bureau, then one of the officers must have it. I'll have to speak with Agent Creagan about it. That could still be considered evidence," he says.

"If you never processed it into evidence and didn't even consider an important, then Creagan doesn't have it. I just spoke to him, and he said he's never heard anything about it. It wasn't inventoried with the other evidence for the case and has never been mentioned. That key belongs to me. It was Greg's, and not only did Greg intend it for me, but he also left his entire estate to me. What he owned, I own now," I say.

"I'll talk to all the officers and see if we can track it down," he says.

"I suggest you look carefully," I say and end the call.

Dragging my duffle bag out of the tiny compartment considered a closet in this room, I start pulling clothes from the dresser drawers as I call Creagan again.

"Do you need me for anything in particular? Is there something specific for this investigation that I need to be doing today or the next few days?" I ask.

"No," he says. "Why?"

"Then I need to take a couple of days away. I'm going back to DC to find that key and see if I can figure out what it means. I'll be accessible, so you can call me if you need anything or if anything in the investigation changes," I say.

"All right, I'll see you when you get back," he says.

I hang up without even knowing if I said goodbye or not. My next call is to Sam.

"You're going back to Sherwood tomorrow, right?" I ask.

"Yes," he says, sounding confused. "Is everything okay?"

"I'm going with you. But can we leave today?" I asked.

"Emma, what's going on?"

"I need to go back to DC. I have to go by headquarters and the police department, then I need to go back to Sherwood for a couple of days. A potentially important piece of evidence from Greg's case slipped through the cracks, and I have to find it. Especially now that I know Lydia was in touch with him because of something having to do with the Dragon. I need to figure this out," I say.

"Let me finish up what I'm doing right now, then I'll come back to the hotel and get packed. We can leave as soon as you want to," he says.

"Thank you," I say. "I love you."

"Love you, too."

He hangs up, and I toss my phone to the bed so I can finish packing up. By the time he gets to the hotel an hour and a half later, I've already stacked clothes for him on the bed and have packed up his toiletries. Which he promptly unpacks so he can take a shower to wash the cornfield off him. Fortunately, he is the quintessential male when it comes to showering and is out, dressed, and ready to go within fifteen minutes.

We hit the road for the few hours it will take to get to the DC area. I call my father on the way. After the long day and a long drive, we'll want to stay the night with him before heading to Sherwood tomorrow.

CHAPTER SIX

It was good to see my father and spend a little time with him. Even if it was just one night. It's been a while since we had a visit of any real length. I've been so wrapped up in everything going on in Harlan, and he has been doing his own investigations, sending us in opposite directions a good bit of the time.

But in a lot of ways, that feels normal. Growing up, I was never sure if I was going to wake up in the morning to both of my parents still in the house like they were when I went to bed. For a while there, I couldn't even be sure I was going to wake up in the same house where I went to bed.

They were always traveling, always going off to work on something I didn't know about. It wasn't until I was older that I understood how important my father's work was. His role in the CIA influenced him to ensure I trained in martial arts from the time I was old enough to kick and not fall over. It kept his eyes sharp, his awareness precise, and his family always moving.

It wasn't until I was an adult that I actually understood why my mother would sometimes leave. As far as I knew when I was young, she didn't work like my father did. She stayed at home with me. Occasionally, she left and would be gone for a few days, but I never questioned it. They never let me feel fear or worry, so I also didn't feel the need to know where she was.

Not until she died. It took another seventeen years for me to uncover the truth. To find out what an amazing woman she actually was, and about all the lives she saved without my ever even knowing it. By then, I had been without my father for a decade. Now that he's back in my life, it's wonderful just to have the option to go see him when I can.

It felt good to settle into my old room, in the house I lived in by myself from the time I was eighteen until he came back. We talked over breakfast, but I didn't venture too far into everything we had been investigating. I didn't want my entire relationship with him to be about work.

Now that I'm back in Sherwood, I kind of wish I had taken that opportunity to see if he had any insights or ideas. I'm sitting in the living room of what was my grandparents' house, but that is now my home. The key I picked up from the police department, after we found it in a little-used corner of the evidence room, flips over and over in my palm as I try to figure out why Greg would have given it to Lydia to give to me.

He didn't tell her what it was for, or why I needed to have it.

It doesn't look like a house key. I wouldn't need it anyway. I've already emptied out Greg's apartment and sold it. All the personal papers his lawyer gave me after the will was probated are spread out on the table in front of me. I've dug through them several times, looking to see if I might have missed a deed or a description of another piece of property.

There is nothing. I don't have any notes, any mysterious letters. No treasure map. There's nothing that gives me any indication of what this key belongs to.

For a brief moment, I wonder if it could have anything to do with the bombing at the bus station when he was still in Jonah's grasp. At the time, nobody knew where he was or what had happened to him. He had been missing for over a year, only to resurface on surveillance footage walking through a bus station in Richmond. He was seen going to the back of the station near the lockers, then walking over to the information desk, then leaving seconds before the entire building exploded.

But the key doesn't look like it fits a locker. And it wouldn't make sense for that to be why he had it, either. We'd already talked about the bombing, and he'd had every opportunity to give me that key himself. I knew he was there for Jonah, which would mean whatever was put into that locker was not intended for me.

I stand up and make my way up to the attic. One corner has been devoted to Greg's belongings that I haven't figured out what to do with yet. Most of his things have already been sold or donated, but the remaining handful that I haven't decided about yet are relegated to the attic. Every now and then, I go up and look at them, waiting for some sign as to what I'm supposed to do with them.

They all have different reasons for being there. For a trunk, four metal boxes, a jewelry box, and a wooden chest, it's all the same reason. They're locked, and I haven't been able to get inside. A couple of them feel very light, as if they may just be empty. But I don't feel comfortable getting rid of them until I know what's inside.

With this key, I might get the answer.

I kneel down in front of the pile of his belongings and reach for the first metal box. It's military green with a silver handle. Not very heavy. It makes no noise when I tilt it back and forth. Resting the box in my lap, I try to put the key into it. It doesn't fit. I flip it over and come at it at different angles, but I can't make it work. Setting that box aside, I move on to the next.

After all of the metal boxes prove to be dead ends, I try the jewelry box. Rocking it back and forth creates a small, dull rattle inside. My heart sinks a little when I think about what might be making that sound. I already knew he was planning to ask me to marry him. A couple of times, he had even given hints that he had chosen the ring.

By the sound, it seems he definitely had.

I've just finished testing the wooden chest when I hear Sam calling from downstairs. His footsteps rattle the stairs coming up into the attic.

"Any of them?" he asks.

I shake my head and roll back from my knees to stand up.

"I tested everything I could find up here with a lock. The key doesn't fit in any of them. Which actually brings to mind another question as to where the keys are for all of these boxes? For a man so meticulously organized as Greg, he seemed to have a problem keeping track of where his keys went," I say.

"Don't all guys?" Sam shrugs.

I rise up on my toes to give him a kiss. "That would be why you have that little keychain that screams when you click the button on the remote."

"Ah," he says, following me as I make my way down the steps. "But you didn't keep in mind the logical fallacy of that, which is that I no longer know where the remote is."

I laugh, shaking my head as I set the key down on the kitchen counter and start the coffeemaker. There are two grocery bags sitting on the kitchen table that weren't there when I went up to the attic. I nod toward them.

"What's that?" I asked.

"You haven't been home for a while, so I thought I would pick up a couple of essentials for you," he shrugs.

I use my fingertip to pull one of the bags open and peek inside. My eyes slide over to him.

"Yeast and brown sugar?" I raise an eyebrow with a teasing grin.

"Cinnamon rolls are essential," he offers. "And I've been doing without them for almost two months. I am dangerously depleted in all of the vitamins and minerals they supply."

"We can't have that. What kind of girlfriend would I be if I let you wallow away without all those essential cinnamon roll nutrients?"

"Well, let's be honest. You'd be the kind that's out solving murders and trying to take down a really messed up secret society. That can be a little time consuming," he says.

I wrap my arms around his neck and kiss him. "I tell you what. I'll make up a few batches and put them in the freezer. That way, all you have to do when you are home and feel the need for a cinnamon roll is pop them out, let them thaw, and bake them."

"I can live with that," he says. I smile and make my way back over to the coffeemaker. "Oh. I forgot to mention, Gabriel says hi."

"Gabriel from the grocery store?" I ask.

Sam pulls a bunch of grapes out of one of the bags and rinses them in the sink before pulling several off and popping them in his mouth.

"Yep. He's been back for a few weeks. I went through his line today, and he asked about you. He said he thought you had started going to a different grocery store," he says.

Laughing, I reach for a couple of mugs. "He thinks I'm cheating on him with a different store? Where? There's only that store and the corner market in Sherwood."

"Long-distance grocery store cheating," he shrugs. "Anyway, I filled him in on what you are up to, and he said to say hi."

"Oh. Well, that's nice. I'm glad to hear he's doing okay. I was worried about him after his grandmother died."

"He seems to be in good spirits."

The grapes go into the fruit bowl on the kitchen table, and he reaches back into the bag. Out comes a package of candy corn, and I shake my head.

"Cinnamon rolls, grapes, and candy corn. All the major food groups," I say.

He peers into the bag. "I bought stuff for chili, too."

CHAPTER SEVEN

A couple of hours later, the chill of the evening has set in enough to justify thick socks with my leggings and a floppy sweatshirt that stretches down to the middle of my thighs. It is my official "fall-at-home" uniform, and I'm beyond thrilled to actually be in it. Memories of the scorching heat of this summer are still lingering with me, and I'm grateful for every cool breeze.

The chili is just about done simmering on the stove as I pull a cast-iron skillet of cornbread out of the oven. The butter and bacon fat melted into the bottom sizzles. It'll form into a sturdy crust on the bread, making it perfect for standing up to the thick chili.

Inverting the pan onto a metal rack, I leave it to cool for a couple of minutes while I ladle big bowls of chili. I sprinkle each one of them with cheese and add spoons before setting them on a tray. The cornbread is still technically too hot for me to slice, but I'm not feeling particularly patient. The house smells warm and full of spices, and I want to bury myself in the food.

Once thick wedges of the bread are added to the tray, I pick it up and head outside. Sam stands beside the fire pit he built me. Flames jump and spark into the night sky. There's something masculine and primal about him building a fire and standing there with a long stick, prodding the flames, to grow. It stirs up all kinds of feelings in me. I have to set the tray down and wrap my arms around him from behind.

My hands flatten on his chest and stomach, and I nuzzle close to the curve of his neck. His clothes smell like smoke, but his skin is all fresh, clean Sam. He pats my hand on his chest and leans back against me, so we prop each other up.

When he's done stoking the flames, he tosses the stick down beside the fire pit, and we pick up our food to carry over to the wooden glider sitting to the side of the fire. One of my grandmother's quilts is already draped across the back, and we nestle down into it, pulling it around our shoulders to ward off the chilly night air.

We eat in silence for a few minutes, just enjoying the sensory layers of the evening around us. The touch of the cold air in contrast to the heat radiating from the fire. The smell of the wood-burning and the spices in the food. The night sounds of birds and insects who still haven't given up but will soon quiet down for winter.

When Sam speaks, his voice sounds almost impossibly loud against the crackling of the flames.

"Can I ask you something?" he asks.

"Of course," I say.

"I haven't wanted to mention it because I don't want to upset you. But I've heard you talk about the Dragon a couple of times. I know he has to do with an undercover assignment you did early in your career with the Bureau, but you've never really given me all the details."

"They aren't the most pleasant details," I tell him.

"Will you tell me anyway?" he asks. "I want to know who this guy is and what's going on with him."

I stare into the dancing fire, finding the shades of color in the flames and against the dark wood turning to pale ash in front of me.

"The Dragon is a man named Darren Blackwell. He was already under investigation by the Bureau for quite a while before I got involved. They had a lot on him, but not quite enough to be absolutely sure of a conviction. He was linked to major drug running and a seemingly never-ending stream of violent crime. There were indications he led organized crime syndicates and instigated street wars to boost his own income. As you can imagine, the Bureau was very interested in not only stopping him but also finding out who was working with him," I explain.

"It could lead to stopping a major vein of drugs and crime," Sam says.

"Exactly. But in order to do that, they needed to get to him in a way that would be unexpected. Just a normal sting wouldn't work. They couldn't send in a fake buyer or somebody pretending to want to work for him. He would figure that out too fast. This guy was smart and influential. Smooth, respected, and feared. They needed something he wouldn't be suspicious about, something he would have to work for. So, they sent me."

"Why you?" Sam asks.

"I was new. I had only been working in the Bureau for a short time, and my face wasn't known in criminal circles yet. That's an unfortunate side effect for some agents who frequently go undercover. Of course, most stay undetected and can do multiple assignments without ever being noticed. But there's always a possibility of criminals from one investigation crossing over into another. They wanted to make sure the person they sent in was a fresh, unrecognizable face."

"And a woman," Sam notes.

"Yes," I say. "That was the point. He already had an army of men ready to do anything he wanted of them. He didn't need anybody else. And he wasn't interested in new customers unless they were highly recommended and came with mind-boggling amounts of money to throw at him. So they came up with a different approach. Dangle something in front of him he couldn't have. He wasn't used to that. He was used to always getting exactly what he wanted, when he wanted it. The only way to get the information the Bureau needed and get close enough to him to bring him down was to earn his trust and loyalty."

"That doesn't sound easy," he says.

"Not at all. And not guaranteed. There was always a possibility he wouldn't be interested. Or he wouldn't be willing to go along with it. Sending me in was a risk, and everybody involved knew it wasn't going to be fast. This wasn't something that I could just do in a few days or a couple of weeks, and it would be over with. That became my life. And I had to live every minute of it," I say.

"What does that mean?" he asks.

"I got a different apartment. A whole new wardrobe. They gave me an acting coach to change my voice and the way I walked. Different makeup. A different car. A fake job. I constructed an entirely separate life, so if he looked into me or had his men follow me and try to find out something about me, there wouldn't be anything unusual for him to notice. That meant I did a lot of the case alone. I didn't have the rest of the team around me all the time. That would have stood out too much."

"You said it was the first case you worked on with Greg," he says.

"It was. They moved him into the building I was living in. A couple of floors down. That way, he was at least in close proximity. We could communicate without its being detected by any of Darren's people. The information I gathered was transferred to Greg, who took it back to the team."

"How long did it take you?" he asks.

"Months. At first, it was all about catching his interest. I made it clear that I wasn't interested in him. I didn't fall for his charm or his lines. I had to make him want me. That was the only way I was going to gain his trust or get into his inner circle. It was far too easy for him to get the attention of pretty much any woman he even looked at sideways. They were disposable to him. But if I could make myself desirable and make him interested enough to work to get me, then I was in."

"And you did," Sam notes.

I nodded, turning back to look into the flames. "It took me a long time. There were days when I thought I'd lost his interest. When he didn't pursue me and was with other women. But he always came back. And then he tested me."

"What do you mean, he tested you?" Sam asks.

"He brought me out with him one night. He never told me who he was or what he did. That was part of his game. I was supposed to be impressed by him just because I was impressed by him. Not because I knew he had power or because of his crimes. But he had to make sure I could be trusted. That I wasn't going to panic and run away at the first sign of something shady."

"What did he do?"

"He brought me along on a drug deal," I say, my throat tightening as I get deeper into the recollections of that night. "He showed me his product and let me test it so I would know how pure and high-quality it was. Then I watched him murder a man."

The words tumble out of my mouth without emotion or filter. I can't try to stop them or pretty them up, or they won't come out. It's a cold reality, a dark spot I carry with me in the inner recesses of my being. It will never go away. Nothing I ever do will change it or absolve it. It is done.

"You couldn't do anything?" Sam asks, reaching a hand to squeeze my thigh comfortingly.

"No," I shake my head. "I had no idea what was coming. I didn't know he was going to try to push me over the edge like that. I was expecting the drug deal. That was a given. One day he was going to show me his business and see how I reacted to it. It would be perfectly easy to just dispose of me if I showed any signs of discomfort or seemed to be a risk. I didn't think he would go as far as murder. It was one of the hardest lessons I ever had to learn."

"What did you do?" Sam asks.

"I went along with it," I say. "What else was I supposed to do? I acted as if it didn't bother me, as if it excited me. If I hadn't, I would have been in that alleyway beside the victim. The next morning, the newspaper probably would have had an article about a prostitute and her john getting mowed down because of a drug deal gone bad. I did what I had to do to survive, and to bring back the information the Bureau needed to take him down."

"What happened to him?"

"The day I met him at the bar, he was planning to take me to the house he bought for us and ask me to marry him. I pulled my gun on him and got him to his knees. The rest of the team came in and arrested him. One of his men had tried to warn him. In the last seconds, his lieutenant had figured out who I was and tried to get him out of there. But Dragon wouldn't go. He chose me over his man. He just wanted to be with me. Or who he thought I was. He was taken to jail, tried, and convicted. Sentenced to multiple life sentences. I had done my job."

"And then?" Sam asks.

"And then, several years later, he was being transferred to a different prison. There was a horrific crash, and when it was all said and done, a corpse was found in the prison transport vehicle. Crushed and burned beyond recognition. He was the only prisoner being transported that day. He was declared dead, and that part of my life was closed," I say.

"It wasn't closed before that?" Sam asks.

"It's hard knowing there's somebody in the world who feels about you the way I knew Darren Blackwell felt about me."

CHAPTER EIGHT

"I have to go to work," Sam whispers in my ear and kisses me on the temple.

Groaning my protest, I roll onto my back, then onto my other side to swing my arm over him.

"No," I whine. "Not yet."

"That's what you've been saying for the last hour," he chuckles. "I really have to go. But I promise I will be back this evening. As soon as I get off work."

I pull myself up so I can press my nose against his and look into his eyes.

"Come home early?" I ask.

"If I can," he says. "Sherwood does still need a sheriff, you know."

I let out a dramatic huff, and he laughs, giving me a sharp, playful smack on my butt. He pulls himself out from under me, and I flop onto the mattress.

"So dramatic," he says with a laugh and heads into the bathroom. "I'm going to take your car into the shop this morning. See if they can figure out why it's making those weird sounds."

"Thank you," I call back.

I reluctantly throw on a bathrobe and shuffle into the kitchen so I can at least make him a travel mug of coffee before he heads out into the chilly autumn morning. I fully intend on spending my day in a sweatsuit and thick socks. Possibly up to my eyeballs in pumpkin tea.

My plan is to go over all of Greg's papers and the pile of stuff in the attic again. I'm not exactly optimistic about getting anything out of that, but it will at least be a warmup for the next part of the plan. That involves pulling out my laptop and opening up the file of old archived emails I never really thought I would look at again.

I kept them because that's what I do. There's really no other explanation than that. Sam hates that my inbox is overflowing. It makes him twitchy. But it's part of my routine. Every couple of weeks, I sit down and organize the countless messages that fill up the inbox day after day. Most of them get deleted, but others are sifted into individual folders and tucked away, where I can't see them, but I know they're there.

These are the emails from my friends and family. Details about cases that I've worked or even just the ridiculous memes Dean insists on sending to me. Some of them, I have to admit, are funny. Others are confusing, and I don't really understand what they're supposed to mean. And then there's that third category, where I can only hope he didn't actually mean to include me in the email list.

What matters is I don't need the vast majority of them; there's really no point in their existing other than the fact that they exist. I don't go back in and read them or revisit them. But I know they're there in case there ever seems to be a reason I would need to read them again.

Like now. I open the folder labeled "Greg" and stare at the pages of communication between us that span the years we worked together. There's a point somewhere in those pages of messages, a fault line, where our relationship shifted. It was never deeply sexy and passionate or even playful and silly. It wasn't like Sam and me.

But it was steady and comfortable. We knew each other well and had fun together. I felt secure around him and knew if there was a future for us to have, it would be just as steady and comfortable.

Maybe nothing that would move mountains, but enough to keep moving forward if the ground moved under us.

A strange kind of emotion settles over me as I scroll back to the very first messages we exchanged. Most of them are brief. Some just a couple of words. Some nothing more than attachments. But there are others that chronicle our slowly growing relationship.

Those are the messages I'm after. I'm several months into our knowing each other when my phone rings. I reach over to it without taking my eyes off the screen and answer.

"Hello?"

"Emma?" Bellamy says.

"Hey, B," I say. "How are you doing?"

"Doing okay. What are you up to?" she asks.

"Believe it or not, I am sitting in my living room reading through all the emails Greg and I ever sent to each other," I say.

"Greg?" she asks. "Greg Bailey?"

"Do I know any other Gregs?" I ask, laughing despite the sadness.

"It's just that…"

"There's a reason behind it," I reassure her. "I'm not just wallowing, and I haven't snapped and started up an email correspondence with myself. He left me this key; there has to be a reason for it. I've gone through every one of his possessions that had a lock on it, but the key doesn't fit any of them. I know it's not to his apartment because it doesn't look like a regular house key. So, I'm at a loss. I figured maybe if I went back through and read all of our emails, maybe I would find something he mentioned."

"Like what?" she asks.

"I'm not sure. Just something. Maybe a property he owns that he forgot to leave a deed for with his lawyer, or a locker in an airport somewhere. I really don't know. But the thing is, there has to be a very important reason he wanted to make sure Lydia gave me this key. He said, "just in case". That meant he was expecting something bad to happen. Or, at least thought it was a strong possibility," I say.

"Do you think he was going to meet with Jonah?" she asked.

"No," I say. "I don't think so. He would tell me about that. There would be no reason for him to go meet with Jonah without letting me or some of the other members of the task force know. The notes that Lydia sent are pretty vague. They just say that she was tracking somebody once referred to as the Dragon and that he might have been responsible for a cold case murder she was looking into."

"What murder? Someone you investigated?" she asks.

"No. Somebody named William Chappell. I never even heard the name. But obviously, she found out something about him that interested her and was looking into it. She stumbled on some association with the Dragon and kept digging. She found out enough to catch Greg's attention and for him to tell her not to get any closer," I say.

"Did he tell her why?" Bellamy asks.

"Not according to her or her notes. She said they were planning to get together later, and she figured they would talk more about it then. Obviously, he never got a chance," I say.

"He knew something. He had the same information the rest of us did. That Darren Blackwell died in that prison transport crash years ago. Why would he be worried about her looking into a potential cold case murder involving him? Unless he knew there were still people associated with Dragon lurking around," she says.

"Or Dragon's not dead," I say.

"How could that be?" she asks.

"I don't know. But it's something to think about. And Greg wanted to make sure I had this key in case whatever he was going to do didn't work out for him. I highly doubt Darren Blackwell was wandering around DC. His face is far too recognizable. He would have been identified immediately. But Greg was meeting somebody out on that beach. And he didn't know if he was coming back."

"Let me know if I can look into anything for you," she says. "I know you're really busy with the investigation in Harlan."

"I will, thank you," I tell her. "But don't get too excited. I highly doubt it's going to be like the last time I asked you to look into things for me, and you got to go on a vacation to Florida."

"Hey," she defends herself. "I got a lot of valuable information during that trip."

"And several lovely pictures of you drinking cocktails with little umbrellas," I say.

"Part of the job," she says. "I was undercover as a tourist."

"You are very convincing," I say. "So, what are you doing for Halloween?"

"Halloween?" she asks.

"I'm ready to just get my mind off all of this. It's only a few weeks away. We should think about doing something fun."

"Really?"

"Yeah," I say.

She makes a sound that is close to a squeal, but as if she's holding it back with her teeth.

"I have so many ideas," she whispers.

"For what?" I ask, already cringing. I love Bellamy to death, but once she gets an idea for some wild project or party or something, there is absolutely no stopping her. I've had to learn to give her a wide berth when she gets into event-planning mode.

"Group costumes!" she says. "Now that Eric and I are together, the two of us and you and Sam can dress up as something."

"We should include Dean, too," I say.

"Alright. How about the guys wear all black, then you and I can wear sparkly green sweaters and skirts with ornaments on them, and we can go as the night before Christmas."

"That seems like it would require some very rigid walking procedures to keep up the theme," I point out. "Anyway, wouldn't that be better if we were doing the Tim Burton version?"

"True," Bellamy says. "Okay, how about the Beatles?"

"There are five of us. What will Dean be?" I ask.

"...a tambourine?"

"I think we need to work on this idea-generating thing a little bit."

"All right. I'll get on that. I'm just excited to think we get to hang out soon," she says.

"Me, too," I say. "It's been a long couple of months."

"I just wanted to check in with you. I actually have to go. Creagan has this super fun way of looking at work that says if he's out in the field doing an investigation, he thinks the rest of us can do three times as much work as we do when he is here at headquarters," she says. "And I don't even work here! I'm just hanging out in Eric's office!"

"That I remember distinctly," I say. "I'll talk to you soon."

Just as I'm hanging up the phone, I hear a crash near the front of the house. It's the distinct sound of breaking glass.

CHAPTER NINE

I pause, my hand hovering over my phone as I listen. I'm in the back of the house, set up in the small room I converted into an office. The crashing sound came from the kitchen, like the glass pane on the back-door smashing.

I get up quietly and move to the door of the office, wanting to check what's going on before I overreact. Of course I've left my gun in the bedroom, and that's across the hall from where I am now. There's no way I can get to it without drawing attention to myself. Opening the door, I step out into the hallway. This would be the point in every horror movie when the person calls out into the empty house, "Hello? Is someone there?"

Never in the history of existence has shouting something like that actually ended well. So, I don't do it. Instead, I open my phone and dial the nine and the one. That way I'm prepared but haven't called emergency responders for another incident of a squirrel throwing a rock through my window. I think the construction was to blame for making them angry.

When I get to the end of the hall, rustling in the living room catches my attention. I head in that direction, and a sudden blast of movement from the side of the room startles me. I don't have a chance to process what I'm seeing before a mass hits me, and I land on the floor. My phone lands by my hand and bounces a couple of feet away. I scramble over to it and hit the other one just before getting a hard kick to the back of my head.

Whoever kicked me either knew exactly what they were doing or didn't know at all because it wasn't enough to cause any serious damage. But it was enough to make consciousness tighten down from the corners of my eyes like a tunnel getting narrower.

I'm only out for a few seconds, it seems. The next thing I know, I feel hands grab me. As they pull me up off the floor, I turn and swing a punch.

"Hey," a familiar voice says. "It's just me. Calm down."

My vision goes clear, and I'm able to focus on the face hovering over me.

"Gabriel?" I ask, blinking away the darkness. "What are you doing here?"

"Are you all right?" he asks.

"Yeah," I say, slowly coming back to my senses. "Somebody was in my house. He kicked me."

Gabriel helps me sit all the way up.

"Are you okay? You think you can stand, or do you need to sit there for a few more seconds?"

"I'm going to sit here," I say. "I called 911; they should be on the way. What are you doing here?"

"I was going down the street to visit a buddy of mine, and I saw a guy burst out through the front door and run down the street. I realized it was your house after I saw him, so I was worried. I came in here to check on you and saw you passed out," he says.

"Did you see the guy clearly?" I ask. "Could you tell who he was?"

Gabriel shook his head. "No. I mean, I could see that he was wearing jeans and a red sweatshirt. That's it. I didn't see his face or anything. Did he just come in here?"

"He broke in through the back door," I say. "I was in my office, and I heard the glass break."

"Where's your car? It doesn't even look as if you're home," he says.

"It's in the shop," I say. "Sam took it in this morning. He must have either already come back for his squad car or had somebody else bring him back by to pick it up while I was in the shower. I've been gone so much, and without the car here, it probably does look as if I'm not here. That would be why he decided to try to break in now."

"Did he get anything?" Gabriel asks.

"I don't think so," I say. "He was only in here for a few seconds, and he just went from the kitchen into the living room. It doesn't look as if he tried to take any of the art or collectibles. The TV hasn't been touched. But, again, he was only in here for a few seconds. He really didn't get an opportunity."

"What about the drawers?" he asks.

I look over and notice the drawers and the sideboard are standing open. Glancing behind me, I notice the drawers in the buffet in the dining room are open, too.

"I don't know," I say.

"Are they like that in the kitchen?" he asks.

"Honestly, I didn't even look in there. When I was coming out of the office, I heard somebody in the living room, so I came this way."

"You sit here," Gabriel says. "I'm going to go check."

He heads into the back of the house and a few seconds later returns, nodding.

"They're all standing open. There's stuff all over the floor, as if whoever it was tossed everything out of a couple of the drawers."

A second later, lights and sirens announce the arrival of the police. Sam rushes in first and drops down in front of me, holding my face in his hands.

"Are you all right?" he asks.

"I'm fine," I tell him. "It just startled me more than anything. Took me by surprise."

"The guy kicked her in the back of the head," Gabriel says. "She was out for a few seconds."

"Seriously?" Sam asks.

I roll my eyes. "I'm fine. My head hurts, but I'll be okay. He didn't aim for any of the really soft places."

Sam takes my hands and helps me up to my feet. He kisses both hands, then holds them to his chest and leans down so he can look into my eyes.

"You will do anything to make me come home from work early, won't you?" he teases.

I laugh. "Absolutely. That was my plan all along. That guy was just from the high school theater department."

Sam kisses me on the forehead and leads me over to the couch so I can sit down. Three EMTs armed with what looks like a mobile hospital packed up into red bags rush inside.

"Guys," I call over. "It's fine. Stand down. There's no blood." I slide my eyes over to Sam and lower my voice under my breath. "There's no blood, right?"

He peeks at the back of my head and shakes his. "No."

"There's no blood," I say, lifting my voice up again.

One of the EMTs, a young man I have encountered a couple of times before, lets out a sigh of relief.

"It's always a concern when we find out we're getting a call involving you," he says.

My mouth opens, but no effective sounds come out, and I close it.

"Thank you, Miller," Sam says. "I appreciate it that you guys rushed out here. Emma seems okay, but I would feel better if you would give her a quick once over. Just to be sure."

I sit on the couch while they shine a light in my eyes and have me follow it back and forth. Another of them presses her fingers into the back of my head to find the tender spot.

"Are you sure you don't want to go to the hospital?" Miller asks.

I shake my head. "No. I'm fine. Not the first time I've been knocked out for a few seconds."

"And probably not the last." He packs up his materials and smiles at me. "Have a good day."

My eyes slide slowly over to Sam as they leave.

"Resounding endorsement of me," I mutter. "Just kind of in general."

"If everything's okay, I think I'm going to go ahead and go," Gabriel says.

Hearing his voice startles me a little. I had almost forgotten he was even in the house. Sam looks over at him and nods.

"Thank you for coming in and helping her," he says.

"She didn't really need my help," Gabriel answers with a smile. "Emma can handle herself."

"She can," Sam agrees. "But that doesn't mean it isn't good to have backup every now and then. If you don't mind, would you stop by the police station whenever you have a chance and make a report?"

He looks a little hesitant. "I didn't really see much. But I'll tell you everything I know."

"Thank you," Sam says. "Sometimes, it seems as if you don't have any information that could be helpful, and it turns out to be critical."

"Thank you, Gabriel," I say. "I really do appreciate you coming in here like that. And it was good to see you."

He smiles. "You, too."

He leaves, and Sam gets up to close the door and lock it.

"Tell me what actually happened," he says.

"I did," I say. "That is exactly what happened. I came out of my office because I heard glass breaking, I heard somebody in the living room, and I got knocked on my ass. Then I started to get up and got kicked in the head. That's really all that happened."

"And you didn't see anything else?" he asks.

"Why are you asking me this?"

"Because you're famous for leaving out details so you can figure things out for yourself."

"That's not what I'm doing this time. My car, as you know, isn't here. It looks as if I'm not home, and I haven't been for weeks. Somebody was probably just watching and thought this was a good opportunity, not realizing that I'm here."

"But what were they looking for?" Sam asks.

I shake my head. "That's the thing. He was only in here for a few seconds. But all the drawers are open. It's as if he came in and just systematically opened every drawer he came across as he walked through the house. He dug through them and tossed stuff out. He was looking for something specific."

"And small," Sam says. "Something that would fit in a drawer."

"Only one thing I can think of might be catching somebody's attention," I say.

"What do you mean?" he asks.

"Maybe it wasn't random," I say.

I get up and go to the kitchen. Running my hand over the counter, I look on the floor, then on the table. I go into my office and search the desk and the carpet.

"What is it?" Sam asks.

"The key," I tell him. "It's gone."

CHAPTER TEN

"Somebody knows what that key is to," I say. "And it was important enough for them to break into my house to get it."

"How could they know?" Sam asks. "You just picked it up from the police."

"I know," I nod. "But it was obviously important. Now I have to figure out not just what it unlocks, but who would want whatever it is enough to steal the key."

"The key was setting on the kitchen counter, right?" Sam asks. "Then why go through the drawers in the other rooms?"

"I don't know. Maybe looking for the same thing I was. Direction."

My phone starts ringing, and I look around, trying to remember where it ended up when I hit the ground. I see it and scoop it up just as it's about to cut off.

"Hello?" I say.

"Griffin? Are you okay? You sound terrible," comes Creagan's voice.

"Today is just a fantastic day for making me feel good about myself," I mutter.

"What?" Creagan asks.

"Nothing," I sigh. "What do you need?"

"I need you to get your ass back here to Harlan," he says.

"Why? Is something going on?"

"Just a hearing tomorrow," he says.

"What hearing?" I ask.

"What's going on?" Sam asks. I shake my head. "It's Creagan," I mouth.

"Xavier Renton," he says.

That's all he needs to say. My eyes light up, and I reach for Sam. He stands up and comes over to me so I can grab onto his shirt and hold it tight to keep me steady.

"He's getting a new trial?" I gasp.

"The decision just came down," Creagan explains. "They're willing to do a hearing tomorrow afternoon to determine the next steps. I think if you're here to speak on his behalf, it could make a major difference. Oh, and while you're here, maybe you'd like to use the search warrant I plan on securing to go to the temple."

I let out a cheer.

"I leave for two days and everything happens," I say.

"Maybe we just needed you out of our way," he cracks.

"What the hell is going on today?" I ask Sam, turning my face away from the phone. "Everybody is just dancing around on me."

"Griffin? Griffin, are you listening?" Creagan asks.

"Yeah, I'm here. Sorry. Tell me what happened," I say.

"Some of the details that Xavier told you turned out to be right. I can't really get into it a whole lot more than that, but it was enough to convince the courts to grant him a new trial, and I'm all but positive I'll be able to get us a search warrant. You need to get back here as soon as you can," he says.

"I thought I was in your way," I say.

"Shut the hell up, Griffin, and get your ass back here."

"Lovely speaking with you, too, Creagan."

I hang up the phone and throw my arms around Sam's neck.

"Can you believe it? They're going to give Xavier a new trial. His hearing is tomorrow. I need to be there to speak for him. I need to be able to tell them that they should release him from the facility until his new trial date," I say.

"Do you think that's best for him?" Sam asks, worry clouding his features.

My face drops slightly. "Why would you ask that? How could you possibly think it would be better for him to stay in jail?"

"He's been in custody a long time, Emma," Sam says. "Maybe he's not ready to be out in the world. And would he be okay in Harlan, where all the power players have knives out for him?"

"So, he should have to stay locked up forever? They captured him and threw him in a cage for something he didn't do. So just because he thinks differently from other people and sees the world in his own way, he should just stay there? Because they stole his freedom from him and altered how he's able to perceive the world around him, that should be his consistent reality now? It should be all he ever knows?"

"You're right," Sam relents. "I'm sorry. That was really insensitive of me, and I shouldn't have said it. I just don't want anything to happen to him. He's been through so much."

"I know. Neither do I."

He looks at me for a few seconds. "What is it?"

"It feels strange leaving here after all this just happened," I say.

"One thing at a time, Emma. You can't stay here hoping you'll figure out the key. I'll take care of that and let you know what I find as soon as I can. They need you in Harlan."

I gather Sam into my arms and hold him close. I don't want to leave again. I want to be right here with him. But the need to finish what I started pulls me away from Sherwood and back to the hotel room I didn't even bother checking out of. Sam will be there soon. A few more days here in Sherwood and then he'll come back to help in Harlan.

I wish he could be there for the hearing. He doesn't know Xavier. He can't speak to his character or how he would manage once out of a facility. I don't want Sam there for Xavier. I want him there for me. But this is something I'm going to have to do on my own.

When I get back to the hotel and unpack, I call Dean. We talk about the whole situation, and by the time I get off the phone, I feel better. The night ahead of me seems long. But soon enough, tomorrow will come.

The next day, I know we won't be standing in front of Sterling Jennings when we go in, but my stomach still twists right before we step through the doors. It took this long for us to be able to secure a time to be in front of another judge. It won't change now. But I wouldn't be able to stand there and face Jennings, knowing what he did, knowing he would snatch away Xavier's chances.

We listen to the lawyer present Xavier's case and outline the new developments. Tension makes the muscles along the sides of my neck and behind my shoulders so tight they hurt. Finally, it's time for the lawyer to present our recommendation and the judge to come to her conclusion.

"I want to be clear here," she starts, her eyes scrolling over notes she has spread in front of her. "I have experience with Mr. Renton. I've seen his behavior and witnessed the difficulty he often has with communication and aligning his thoughts with the world around him. It is my understanding that before he was incarcerated, he received a considerable amount of assistance from friends, including Andrew Eagan."

Xavier draws in a deep breath that seems to drag him up a few inches, then he deflates. He looks over at me. I can see the expression in his eyes. The anxiety is creeping up. He wants to say something, but he's struggling to hold it back.

"It's alright," I whisper. "You're going to be alright."

"The lights," he whispers back. "They're too much."

I glance up and, for the first time, notice the intensity of the overhead lighting. It has always been bright. That's just part of the courtroom. But now I'm seeing how stark the lights are. Even more intense than the fluorescent lights in the visiting room at the facility where I see him.

"I know," I tell him. "They're a lot. But you can get through this." I think for a few seconds and something comes into my mind. "Pretend you're in a vending machine. All the lights are surrounding you. Now, which one of those snacks is choosing you?"

He draws in a breath and left it out slowly.

"Pop Rocks," he says.

"Which one do you *want*, though?" I ask. "Tell yourself to be not what chooses you, but what you want. I know a potato chip would probably choose me earlier. Breakable, salty. But I would rather the cookie want to be me. So, I'm being resilient and flexible."

He nods.

"Excuse me. Ms. Griffin, I'm in charge of this hearing," the judge says.

I look around Xavier to her.

"I apologize, your honor. Xavier is feeling anxious, but we have it under control," I say.

"Do you, Mr. Renton?" she asks.

"Yes," Xavier says, nodding. He looks stronger now. "I'm ready to continue."

"Good. As I was saying, some of what I've seen of Mr. Renton concerns me. While I understand his intelligence is considerably above average, he has challenges with perception and basic life functioning that make me wonder if he will be able to assimilate into life outside of the structure of the facility," she says.

"Yes, we understand that, your honor," the lawyer says. "Which is why we came up with the plan we presented. I believe it will properly respect Mr. Renton's rights while also giving him the opportunity to grow accustomed to the world he will be living in again, once his new trial proves his innocence."

"And you are in agreement with this plan?" the judge asks, her eyes moving to the side of the table.

Dean stands, adjusting his suit jacket. He gives a firm nod. "Yes, your honor."

CHAPTER ELEVEN

"Thank you for agreeing to be my handler," Xavier says to Dean as we walk out of the courtroom.

"That's not what I am," Dean says.

"Yes," Xavier says. "It's exactly what you are. You're going to live with me and help me do all the things I'm supposed to do every day while I get used to the world again, so I don't wander off or fall apart. Because apparently, that's what the judge believes I will do."

"I hate the way she was talking about you," I say. "All of them. They were all acting as if you can't function, as if you can't get through a day without someone there to help you."

"Why does that upset you?" Xavier asks.

"Because it's not right," I say.

"And what if it is?" he asks.

We stop in the foyer of the courthouse, and I turn to look at him. He's not in the jail-issued clothes I've always seen him wearing when I visit. His suit is a little too big, hanging on him thanks to his body's not being what it was when he first went to prison so many years ago.

"But it's not," I say. "It's not true. You can function just fine. You're brilliant, Xavier."

"I know that, Emma," he says, his voice steady and strong. "Intelligence has nothing to do with it. I see the world very differently from other people around me. That doesn't scare me. Or hurt me. That's how I've always been. And it makes some things more difficult for me. It's not wrong or something to be upset about. It just... is. When you spoke to me in the courtroom, were you making fun of me?"

I'm taken aback by the question. "No, of course not. I thought it would help calm you down."

"Then you understand," he says.

I'm flustered and not sure how the conversation got this far out of my grasp.

"I understand you think about things in a different way. Some things make you feel better that other people wouldn't understand. But the way they were talking about you... it's as if they think you can't do normal things for yourself. As if you can't just live without someone helping you," I say.

I feel strangely protective of Xavier. The way the judge and the opposing lawyer talked about him felt insulting, but it doesn't seem to bother him. I don't understand how it can be so easy for him.

"Have you ever built yourself a house, Emma?" he asks.

"No," I say, feeling us starting down one of his spirals that I'm going to have to take hold of and ride until it finds an end.

"But you are smart and capable. You are strong and skilled."

"Not at carpentry," I admit.

"And if you were stranded out in the wilderness with only yourself to rely on you wouldn't know where you were or what would happen to you, but you would need shelter. How about then?"

"I could probably put something together," I say. "But it wouldn't be good, like a real house."

"But it would protect you. It would cover your head and be a basic shelter?"

"Yes," I nod.

"And you may feel a little uneasy about it and wish someone who knew better could help you?" he asks.

"Yes," I say.

"So not *can't*. Just harder. The world is made for people who see what you do. I can do those things. But they aren't the way you would do them. And I often wish there's somebody there who knows better who can help me. Not *can't*, Emma. Just harder."

Tears fill my eyes unexpectedly. I try not to show them, but Xavier immediately notices. His eyebrows knit together, and I shake my head.

"I'm fine," I say, waving him off.

"No, you aren't. Why are you crying?" he asks.

"I hate that the only way they would let you out before your trial is if Dean agreed to be with you all the time," I sigh. "You've been locked up for so long. You deserve to just live."

"There's no reason to cry for me. You don't have to be upset that I don't experience life the same way you do. I'm not upset that you don't experience life the way I do. I'm sure there aren't a lot of carpenters out there crying because you can't build a house. So, don't cry because I have trouble making phone calls or telling directions, or interacting. I'm glad Dean will be there with me. I trust him. You trust him. The world is a different place from when I went in. I'm already working at a deficit. But I won't be alone. And I'll be fine."

"Absolutely you will," Dean smiles, throwing his arm around Xavier's shoulders. "I'll be there to make sure of it."

I wait for Xavier to flinch away from Dean's touch, but he doesn't. He's comfortable with him. Maybe this is going to work out after all.

Xavier looks ahead of us to the doors. Sunlight streams in through the glass, and I can see people walking in both directions down the sidewalk. I watch him watching it, his eyes tracing their movements back and forth.

"Are you ready for this?" I ask.

It's the first time he will walk outside without shackles around his wrists and ankles, without somebody holding onto a chain and forcing him along.

Xavier takes a deep breath, then nods. "I'm ready."

We cross the lobby and push through the large glass doors out into the deep, buttery sunlight of the October afternoon. He walks a few paces away from the building and hesitates at the top of the stone steps leading down onto the sidewalk. A few people pass him, and his head snaps to each one as if he's trying to watch every one of their movements.

He takes a few steps down, then retreats. He gets close to the handrail and stops again. He looks lost, as if he doesn't know what to do. Without a word, Dean rushes forward and stands beside him. He touches his hand to the center of Xavier's back. For a moment, they just stand there together, and I notice Xavier's breaths slow, his shoulders relaxing.

They walk down the rest of the steps together, Dean guiding Xavier with no more than his presence beside him.

And suddenly, I understand the difference.

"Are you hungry?" I ask Xavier once I've rushed down the steps to catch up with them on the sidewalk.

"I am," he says. "What time is it?"

"It doesn't matter," Dean says.

Xavier looks at him strangely. "It doesn't matter?"

"No," I say. "It doesn't matter. You don't have to eat on a schedule anymore. You eat when you're hungry." What I said hits me, and I look at him with a concerned expression. "It doesn't matter, does it? Or do you like your schedule?"

He shakes his head. "Not particularly."

"Good," I say. "What are you hungry for? What sounds good?"

His lips press hard together, and he looks around.

"What's wrong?" Dean asks.

"Nothing," Xavier says. "I'm just not used to having so many options. It's been a long time since I've just been able to pick something to eat."

"Isn't that a good thing?" I ask. "Don't you like being able to choose?"

"You have to understand," he says. "It's like having a box of markers. The rest of the world has four. Maybe eight. I have fifty. It's easy to decide when only one option fits. It's much harder when so many could work. I don't know what color fits best when I have so many. I don't know what to choose."

"So, don't," Dean offers. "Don't choose. We will take you to every place you want to go and get you everything that sounds good."

"Absolutely," I say. "We'll get a little bit of everything and have a giant celebratory banquet."

Xavier smiles. "I'd like that."

When we get to the row of restaurants that stretches down one of the biggest streets of town, I park so we can walk from option to option. I notice Xavier staring at people as we pass by them.

"What's fascinating you so much?" I ask. "The clothes?"

"They're talking to themselves," Xavier says.

I look at the group that just passed him by and notice one of them with a phone in his hand and a wireless earbud tucked into one ear.

"No," I say. "He has a headset on. He's talking on the phone."

"Oh," he says with a note of disappointment in his voice.

I laugh. "They had those headsets before you went into prison. Don't you remember them?"

"Not really," he shrugs. "I guess I didn't pay that much attention to people. I rarely used my phone. I lost it a lot. Didn't need it for much. If Andrew couldn't get in touch with me, he just came to my house."

He stops, and I see a look of worry flash over his face.

"What?" Dean asks.

"My house. What happened to it?"

"It's fine," Dean says. "I talked to the courts and your attorney from before you went in. The trust you set up has been maintaining the house. Your bank accounts are fully accessible. You can go home."

A smile nudges the corners of his mouth up just slightly, as if he is almost afraid to show the emotion he is feeling.

"Home," he says softly, the word sounding as if he hasn't said it in a long time and is trying it out.

"Come on," I say, heading for the door of the first restaurant. I hold the door open for him, and as he walks past, a thought occurs to me.

"Xavier, you didn't tell me. What snack did you choose? So you weren't feeling like Pop Rocks?"

"A Swiss Roll," he grins. "Solid and reliable on the outside, and no one can see what's inside. With a nice swirl."

He follows Dean the rest of the way inside.

I give a sharp nod. *And there you go.*

CHAPTER TWELVE

The three of us pile into my hotel room to eat the massive spread of food we picked out. Dean will take Xavier back to his house tonight and give him a chance to decide if he really wants to stay there. He seems to be genuinely looking forward to going home, but I know there's a chance it won't feel right once he gets there.

After all, it's where Andrew died. It's where his entire life went off the rails. And it's been sitting there for a decade waiting for him. The trust he set up before he reported for his sentence ensured the house would be taken care of and properly maintained. The trustee reassured Dean everything is in good shape, but it's still going to take some getting used to.

I've already reserved another room in the hotel, so there's somewhere available for him in case he doesn't feel comfortable.

It's good to see him starting to relax, sampling all the different foods he picked out, and relishing his ability to pick up the TV remote and change the channel at will. We're finishing up when I notice my phone flashing with a new text message. I must not have heard the alert. Wiping my hand on a napkin to get the sticky apricot sauce I put on my spring rolls off, I then pick up the phone.

As soon as I read the message, I'm on my feet.

"What is it?" Dean asks. "Is something wrong?"

I shake my head, forcing the last bite of food down my throat as fast as I can so I can talk.

"No. Not wrong at all. The search warrant went through. I can get back into the temple," I say.

"Let's go," Dean says.

"You'll have to stay here," I tell Xavier.

"Why?" he asks. "I want to see it."

"I know that," I say. "But you're not in law enforcement. Dean is a private investigator, but he was hired by Detective White as a consultant for the case."

"I've waited so long to see that place," he says, anger bubbling just below the surface of his voice. "I only ever saw through other people's eyes. I could only see what Andrew saw. Sterling, Graham Nelson. I only knew what their eyes would show me; I can't do that anymore. I need to see for myself."

He's getting anxious, but there's nothing I can do. It was already a challenge to get the search warrant. I can't compromise it by bringing in not only a civilian but someone directly involved in the case. Not until I run it by Creagan and get permission.

"I will take pictures. I can video call you," I say. As soon as the words are out of my mouth, I realize how ridiculous they are. "No, I can't."

"He doesn't have a phone," Dean says. "That's something we have to fix, and we've got to get you out of that suit. You can't be comfortable just hanging out like that. Give me just a minute."

He leaves the room, and Xavier stares at me. It's uncomfortable, and yet at the same time, I don't want to move. I'm as curious to find out what he sees when he looks at me as he is to see it.

"Don't be afraid for me, Emma," he finally breaks the silence.

"I can't help it," I sigh. "What if I can't do it? What if I can't prove what actually happened and they send you back?"

"Then I would have gotten this time," he says. "This is my reality now. That was my reality then. And if it becomes my reality again, that will be the way it is. I will hang onto now and know that then won't be forever. There's more. I don't want to go back. And I don't believe I will."

"You don't?"

"No. You will do this, Emma. You will understand. It's all just waiting for you. It's always waited for you," he says.

"What do you mean?" I ask.

"There is an explanation for everything. I have waited all these years because it wasn't time. I've been waiting for you," he says.

"How do you know?" I ask, feeling the weight and significance of his trust heavy in my chest.

"You've never looked through me. Other people act as if I don't exist. They try to force me into their world, their language. You weren't afraid to come into mine. Which means you won't be afraid of theirs."

His eyes break away from mine only when the door opens again, and Dean comes back in. Xavier said I have never looked through him, but it's the way he looks at me that's unnerving. I feel he's seeing something other people don't. And I can't help but wonder what it is.

"Try these," Dean says, tossing a pair of sweatpants and a t-shirt onto the bed next to Xavier. "They're probably going to be a bit big on you, but they'll be way more comfortable."

"I will pick up some clothes for you on the way back," I tell him. "Is there anything else you need?"

"A green toothbrush," he says.

It's matter of fact, and I don't question it.

"Stay here and relax," I say. "Don't leave the room. Lock the door when we leave, put the chain on."

"Should I stay?" Dean asks.

"I'll be fine," Xavier tells him. "I do very well staying in one room behind a locked door."

I'd already changed out of my court clothes when we first got back to the hotel, so all I need to do is put on my shoes, and Dean and I are on our way. My heart pounds heavily in my chest as we drive toward the temple. We are going to be able to find them now. All the answers that were hidden.

We will get the proof we were trying to give them all along. And finally, this will be done.

"What do you mean, *nothing?*" Xavier asks two hours later when we're back in the hotel room. "How could there be nothing?"

"That's what we want to know too," I sigh. "We got inside, and when the locksmith opened the doors, the rooms were empty. I mean, there was still furniture, but the papers were gone. The ledgers, the books, the records. The clock on the wall. The wheel. Everything. It was gone."

Xavier shakes his head for several seconds, as if he's juggling the words around in his brain and hopes they will fall together in an order that makes more sense.

"You said everything was there."

"It was," I say. "I have pictures of it."

"Then why can't those pictures be used?" Xavier asks. "Why haven't you shown them to the detective, so he'll open an investigation into Sterling?"

"Because they're not admissible," I explain. "Neither are the ones that Lakyn took. We were both trespassing when we took those pictures. Breaking and entering. A whole slew of crimes was being committed when we took those pictures. That means we can't use them. According to the detective, those pictures don't even exist. Unless he is able to find that evidence in the building when he's there, it doesn't matter."

"What I don't understand is how they got everything out," Dean says. "That building has been under total surveillance for months. The task force has been on twenty-four-hour watch. Nobody has gone in or out. How did that happen?"

"There has to be some other way to get in the building," Xavier announces. "A door that isn't a door."

"What do you mean?" I ask.

"A diversion. They made themselves invisible, so no one would see them. They were there, and they weren't there. They were gone, and they were always gone," he says.

"So, we're right back to the beginning," I say.

"What are we going to do?" Dean plops dramatically against the couch.

"Until we can figure out how they got into that building, we need to know everything we can about The Order of Prometheus. And that means FireStarter," I say.

I pull out my phone and pull up the images I took in the temple the night Dean and I went in. "Look at these letters. They keep track of all the property The Order owns or controls."

"What does that have to do with FireStarter?" Dean asks. "I know they own the cornfields and the Halloween attractions."

"Yes," I nod. "The cornfields adjacent to the ones filled with bones. FireStarter is a shell company, a front for The Order. Look." I open my computer and bring up the file full of research I already did on the mysterious company.

"So, all of these things are business ventures by Prometheus?" Dean asks.

"Not all of them," Xavier points. "They would spread out. Like water on air. If they were too close, you could see them like the mist. So close, the connection would be obvious. But if they stay just so far apart, they would become invisible. If the water is far apart, you can't see it. But it's still there."

"Sterling Jennings' brother is not a member of The Order. Yet, he controls FireStarter," points out Dean.

"And I'm still sure Millie knows so much more than she's talking about," I say. "I think it's what she wanted to tell me. She said she needed to tell me something about her brother. That I needed to stop him."

"But which brother?" Dean asks.

"I don't know," I say. "I thought it had to be the judge. But now that I'm looking at this..." my voice trails off as I look over the list of properties and holdings Eric was able to dig up for me and compare them with the ledgers I found in the Prometheus office.

"What is it?" Xavier asks.

"FireStarter is listed as owning the cornfields and the attractions nearby. The corn maze, the pumpkin patch. All of that is owned by FireStarter. Then the cornfields where all the bodies were found are contested land. They aren't technically owned by anyone, which is how no one is being directly held responsible for the bodies yet. But look at this."

Both men lean around to look at my screen as I hold a fingertip to the image on my phone and then to the screen of my computer.

"There's another property," Dean points out.

"Exactly," I say. "FireStarter is listed as owning those particular pieces of land. But the Prometheus ledger shows *they* own property near the area of that cornfield."

"It just says 'property'," Dean points out. "All these other ones are specific. The temple, a house, a restaurant. But then it just says 'property'. Could it be talking about the cornfield? Would they have not specified what it is so that they could hide it?"

"No," Xavier says. "They wouldn't leave themselves exposed. Like a wire. They would—they would thread it through something else to protect it. So it could go unnoticed. Underground. Something in the same shape, made to bury it in one spot and come out in another."

"Like a conduit?"

Xavier nods. "Two ends of the same thing in two different places."

"You're right. The location numbers are different," notes Dean, crouching low to double-check the discrepancy between my phone and computer. "Do we have a map of the area so we can triangulate this?"

I pull out all of the papers I brought back to the hotel so I could continue researching. One of them is an aerial map of the entire area drawn up to show the contested land. Xavier points out the corn maze, then the field of bones. The listing in the ledger is several hundred yards away and at a diagonal. He shows how their relationship to each other coordinates with the layout of the land and is able to identify the space referenced in the ledger.

"See, nothing's there," Dean says. "It's just an empty space. It's not near that house. It's just space."

"So, why doesn't it say farmland?" Xavier asks. "Or woods?"

I stare at it for a few more seconds and swallow hard.

"Because this is exactly what they mean. Property. This isn't talking about a building or the land. This is a person."

CHAPTER THIRTEEN

TEN YEARS AFTER DEATH ...

Her face had long since become a memory. It would never be forgotten. But that was the problem. It didn't just fade away. It didn't become nothingness. Her face was gone now. Melted, liquefied, pulled to leather, and sunken in the bone. It was nothing.

And yet, out there, beyond the covering and above the dirt, where there was still sunlight and wind, moonlight and stars, more than just raindrops and snowmelt, her face was everywhere.

Ten years, people kept saying. Ten years and nothing.

Ten years and nothing but questions.

Ten years and nothing but questions with no answers.

But there were answers. More answers than there were questions. None of them true. All of them crafted, conjured, imagined. Some made people feel better. Some worse.

None of them told her secrets.

Her face was gone, and yet it was everywhere. And that was the problem.

Ten years is a long time, and yet not long enough to be forgotten.

That should have been the way it worked out. It should have been so easy. Just let it go. Let it go away, and all would be forgiven. All would be released.

Her face was a reminder. Not really of her. Not of when she smiled or laughed or breathed.

It was a reminder of oxygen depleting and neurons firing in one final blast. Of no more heartbeat and blood pooling where it stopped. Of a body raging against nothingness. Against the eternal, final dark.

That face represented something completely different now. Just lies. So many lies.

The lies scattered people. Her face everywhere reminded some they should be looking. For others, it meant to never look again. After all, she was somewhere else. Laughing, smiling, everything behind her, so she could just live.

But, of course, that wasn't true.

No matter how many people thought they saw it. No matter how many stories were told or absolute assurances given.

For some, it brought comfort. For others, anger. For others, confusion.

But it brought none of them to her.

Her face everywhere reminded them it had been ten years.

It brought attention to the other face that kept appearing beside hers. So much good in those eyes.

Ten years of rain, cold, heat, and bugs. Ten years of losing everything that was her.

And no one knew she was there.

There were people all around. She was never alone.

But none knew she was there, just yards away.

If only they had looked a little harder.

CHAPTER FOURTEEN

"I need to go talk to Lilith Duprey," I say.

"Haven't you already talked to her?" Dean asks.

"A few times," I acknowledge. "But I have to again. The house she owns was rented to a member of Prometheus. Now she lives on a piece of land right next to where Prometheus lists owning property, and where FireStarter owns a huge segment of land."

"It's entirely possible she moved into that house, met members of Prometheus, and mentioned she was looking for somebody to rent her house. They knew of Mason, so they connected them. It could be that easy an explanation," Dean says.

"It could be," I say. "I hope it is."

"But you don't think so," Dean observes.

I look into his eyes for a few seconds and let out a long breath.

"I'm coming with you this time," Xavier pipes up. "No reason I can't, right?"

"No," I tell him.

"You're going to where she was, aren't you?" he asks.

"Lakyn?" I ask. "Yes. We will be near there."

"I—I want to see it," he says.

I hesitate. My eyes slide over to Dean, and he shakes his head slightly, but not with enough commitment to be completely rejecting the idea.

"Are you sure?" I ask. "It's pretty disturbing out there."

"Don't you think I see it every day?" he asks. "Don't you think it's in my nightmares? Every night, as soon as I close my eyelids? Don't you think I see everything you told me? She was there because of me, Emma. I didn't kill her, but if she had never met me, she would be alive."

"You can't think that way," I say. "You can't do that to yourself."

"It's not something I'm doing to myself," he replies. "I can't create reality. Not anyone else's, anyway. But I can tell you it's the truth. She listened to me when I told her what was happening. She believed me. She took my tangled mess and unraveled the truth. And she was willing to do whatever she could to prove my innocence. That meant unveiling The Order, and she came so close. She died for it."

"Then I guess it's my fault," I say.

"What do you mean?" he asks. "You didn't even know her. There's nothing you could have done."

"But you said I was here because this has been waiting for me. That you have been waiting for me. If that's true, she died so that I would come," I say.

The words taste bitter on my tongue and make my stomach feel queasy, but I need him to hear it. I can't let Xavier torment himself over Lakyn's death. What she did was her choice. She didn't deserve it. She was doing something incredibly courageous and selfless. But it won't be in vain. And I won't allow Xavier's life to be lost for it, too.

"You aren't to blame, Emma."

"And neither are you," I say.

"I still want to see where she died," he says. "I need to see it. I need to put those nightmares away. I need to brush away the worst parts; the parts my mind keeps showing me. I need to unravel it and see the truth. Like she did for me. So I can say goodbye. I never got that chance."

I want to discourage him, but I can't force him to stay. This is a piece of his life. He deserves to experience it.

Xavier is silent as we drive toward the cornfield. He never stops moving. His head sways from side to side slowly, his eyes moving to cover every inch of the windows and windshield. He's taking it all in, scanning each pixel of reality so he can commit it to memory.

"I've been here before," he suddenly says.

"You have?"

"Yes," he nods. "I didn't know where I was or why. But we drove by here."

"You and Andrew?" I ask.

"Me and Millie Haynes," he says.

My breath catches in my throat. "Millie? Sterling Jennings' sister?"

"Yes," he says. "I loved her once, but she's forgotten me now."

I'm dying to know more, but we've gotten to the cornfield, and the expression on Xavier's face has totally changed. He's not distant anymore, not behind a misty veil of thought and memory. He's locked in place. He looks on edge, as if he's going to climb out of the car in the next few seconds, whether I'm stopped or not.

I bring my car to a stop at one of the carefully placed markers positioned on the field. They were put in those specific places so that no vehicles drove over sections of the grid that hadn't yet been examined. Two officers stand guard to prevent anybody from getting too close to what is still a very active crime scene.

Most of the grid has been examined by now. But there are still sections to go, and as much as all of us hope the cornfield has already given up all its bodies, I feel the chances of that are slim to none.

"Evening, Agent Griffin," Officer Parks says as I approach. "Is there something I can do to help you?"

"Just here to see something," I say.

He steps out of the way, and I gesture for Dean and Xavier to go in front of me. The two officers try to watch us over their shoulders as we move into the cornfield. The stalks have been carefully cut down to clear the ground for the grid. But as we move farther away, it's harder for them to watch us without turning all the way around. Soon, they give up.

I silently lead Xavier toward the back of the field. I don't need any guidance or even time to stop and evaluate where I am. I'll never forget my way to this spot.

It's so different now than it was the night Dean and I followed Lakyn's voice to come here, as if she was haunting us while she was still alive. We finally get to the blackened patch of growth. Her body killed everything trying to grow there. But next year, the land will flourish.

"This is where she was?" Xavier asks quietly.

I nod. "Yes."

"You mentioned there was a cage over her," he says.

"There was," I say. "It was the only thing that kept the animals from tearing her apart." I cringe. "I'm sorry."

"Don't be. That's their way. They can't help it. They didn't know her, and she wasn't even her by the time they came. Which is why I wonder who put that cage there," he says.

"We don't know," I say. "The cage was processed, but there wasn't any interesting evidence on it. No DNA or fibers or hairs."

"Was it heavy?" he asks.

"The cage?" I ask.

"Yes. Was it heavy?"

"No," I say. "It wasn't much stronger than chicken wire."

He nods slowly. "Interesting."

His head tilts to the side, and he turns slightly, rotating his body so his head is almost upside down and his hip faces toward where the body once lay. He's still staring at the ground. It looks like he's trying to figure something out. He stands up and points across the field.

"She came from that direction," he says.

"How do you know that?" I ask.

He stands in the contorted position again and points at the blackened area on the ground. It's not quite the outline of her body, but by the way he points at it, it makes the recognizable shapes stand out.

"The way the plants died. Where her body fluids were pooled. Saturation. They would be heaviest where her internal organs were, and then her mouth and nose. That means most likely this is where her torso was, and this is where her legs were."

"That's right," I nod. "That's exactly how she was lying when I found her."

"Most likely, she was dragged across the cornfield," he says. "She wasn't going to give in easily. It was her way. Her nature. She would fight."

"Yes," I say. "There wasn't really enough of her left to perform an autopsy, but the medical examiner was able to do some examination on the body. She had numerous defensive wounds and injuries consistent with being dragged forcibly."

"Exactly," he nods. "So, she was being dragged across the field, after they were—," he chokes back emotion, "—they were done with her."

I reach a hand to touch his shoulder. He takes a deep breath and continues.

"They just tossed her down. She would tumble to the side that was most natural for her body makeup. If she was lying this way, she fell from that spot," he points and drags his finger to another direction. "Which means she came from that direction."

"That's incredible," I tell him, my mouth hanging open. "I never would have put that together."

"You would have," he says. "I just saved you some time."

"Do you want a minute?" I ask.

He looks at me and nods. Dean and I walk away, heading further down the row. The evidence flags in this area of the cornfield are nowhere near as dense as they were closer to the middle and on the farther side. I resist the urge to watch him.

Standing quietly, I become aware of the sounds around us. They are distant, but I can hear screams and shouts from the corn maze. It's active now, awake in the Halloween season. I have to ask myself how many of the people exploring through the meticulously groomed and shaped maze came just for the proximity to the killing field.

We've already talked to the owner of the maze. He knows the critical importance of keeping anybody who might come to his maze away from the cornfield. We have the officers stationed near the active part of the grid but also have an officer over at the maze. The owner put up additional barriers around the edge to prevent people from going through and trying to sneak over.

Even so, I have no doubt there are plenty of thrill-seekers eager to catch a glimpse at the horror that has been on every news channel in the area for weeks.

Several minutes pass before Xavier comes toward us.

"Are you okay?" I ask.

"Yes," he says. "Thank you for that. For bringing me here."

"Of course," I say.

He looks around, seeming to admire the layout of the grid and the evidence flags.

"What are those?" he asks, gesturing toward one of the bright pink flags.

"We put those in every place where we found anything at all. A bone fragment, a tooth, a piece of cloth, a shoe, a piece of jewelry. Anything that could possibly have to do with one of the people who ended up here, we mark it."

He looks around again, and his eyes catch something in the distance.

"How about that?" he says, gesturing toward the lone flag around twenty feet away.

"That was a grave," I say.

He walks toward it, stopping several inches away from the edge and leaning so he could look down into the roughly hewn hole.

"Who was in here?" he asks.

"The body hasn't been identified yet," I say.

"But it was just one body?" he asks.

"Yes," I nod. "Fairly well intact."

"And no parts of others?" he asks.

"No," I tell him. "Why?"

"It doesn't fit the puzzle," he says.

"The—puzzle?" Dean frowns.

"Look around you. You've marked every puzzle piece you found. Scattered all across this field. Even Lakyn would have been scattered too if it wasn't for that cage. So, why a grave? Doesn't fit the puzzle."

CHAPTER FIFTEEN

I take note of Xavier's comment, folding it up and tucking it away in a little pocket in my mind where I've learned to keep things he says. They don't always make sense when he first says them. In fact, they almost never make sense when he first says them. But if I leave them there long enough, I start to understand.

But I don't have the time right now. I have to go talk to Lilith. It's getting late, and I need to make sure I can get to her tonight.

"Come on," I say. "It's time to go to Lilith's house. It's just over here."

Xavier isn't moving. But he's not looking at the grave anymore. Instead, his head is tilted toward the sounds of the screams and laughter coming from the corn maze, his expression one of concentration. He looks at me.

"What is that?" he asks.

"People going through the maze," I tell him.

"It's open?" he asks.

"Yeah," I say. "I figured they would close this year because of everything that's going on, but they didn't. There's a maze and a pumpkin patch. The patch is probably closed now because it's dark, but that's when people like to go through the corn mazes."

"I want to go," he says.

Shocked by the assertion, I stare at him for a few seconds. I'm waiting for him to tell me he's joking, and we do not quite understand what's funny about it. But he looks completely serious.

"You want to go through the corn maze?" I ask.

He nods. "I haven't been through one since I was just a little boy."

"I'm not so sure it's a good idea," I start. "There are a lot of people and scare actors. It can get really confusing in there."

"Come on, Emma," Dean chimes in. "It's Halloween. Let him have some fun. I doubt things are very festive in the jail at Halloween."

"We aren't even allowed costumes," Xavier says.

There isn't a hint of humor on his face. He says it as if it's a travesty against nature, one of the miseries he suffered. I can't help but commiserate with him at least a little bit. Halloween has always been one of my favorite times of the year. I might not have thrown on a cape and gone trick-or-treating in a long time, but it's hard to imagine not having any celebration at all.

"I'll go with him," Dean says. "You don't need us there, anyway. She'll probably respond better to just talking to you, anyway. Just meet us over at the maze when you're done."

"Okay," I say. "It shouldn't take too long."

Xavier is already off on his way across the field toward the corn maze. Dean rushes after him, and I watch them until they've disappeared into the distance before I turn and head to Lilith's house. It's not too far away from the corn maze. Just through a thicket of woods that separates the tracts of property.

This is far from the first time I've visited the little house. I've tried to talk to Lilith a few times before, but she has been reclusive, not wanting anything to do with the situation. Everyone says they can't blame her. The idea of living that close to something so gruesome is horrifying. Especially for a single woman living alone in such an isolated area. She doesn't want to be involved.

But I think she already is.

I walk up onto the porch and knock on the door. It takes several seconds before she opens it and looks out at me. Her shoulders droop.

She looks less than delighted to find me on her porch. But she doesn't immediately close the door.

"Agent Griffin," she says. "What are you doing here?"

"I'm sorry to show up without calling, Mrs. Duprey, but I'd really like to talk to you for just a minute. Can I come inside?"

I haven't been inside her house before. Every time I've come to talk to her, she has come outside and stood on the porch or down in her yard with me. But I want to get inside. I want to see what her house is like. I don't know why, but something draws me into it.

She hesitates but eventually steps back and gestures for me to come in. I step through the door and into the tiny cabin. It is nothing more than one large room, a kitchen in an alcove to the back, and a bathroom. For one person, it's everything she needs, but it seems strange.

Especially considering what Lydia told me about her.

"Would you like to sit down?" she asks, gesturing toward a sofa up against one wall.

"Thank you," I say.

I sit, and she lowers herself into a wooden rocking chair to the side of the couch.

"I've already told you everything I know," she says. "I don't know what else I can help you with."

"Lilith, I know I've come to talk to you a few times, and other people have, too. We really appreciate your being willing to talk to us. I think you could help more," I say.

She shakes her head, her eyes wide. There's discomfort in that expression, something close to fear.

"I don't know how," she sighs. "I'm just a widow on my own. Just out here by myself. I don't know anything about that cornfield or anybody who might have used it. After my husband passed, I decided to come out here to live, and I was told that land isn't a part of my property. I never knew who it belongs to. Anything past those trees is off-limits to me, and I stay away."

"And you never set foot on it?" I ask.

"No," she says. "I don't really go far from my house very often. I'm just a poor old widow; I stay around here and keep to myself."

"But it hasn't always been that way, has it?" I ask.

"What do you mean?"

"You didn't always live out here. You own that house in Salt Valley," I point out.

"Yes," she says. "I lived there with my husband."

"And before that, you lived in the city," I say. "Right?"

She shifts a little, seeming uncomfortable with a question. "Yes."

"So, you're comfortable around people. Used to it."

"When I lived in the city, I was young. Married. I wasn't an old widow suddenly by myself. It's a very different thing," she says. "And it's terrifying to find out I'm so close to a place where so many monstrosities occurred. I don't get anywhere near that place, especially now that I know what happened there. I won't go past the shed."

I nod and stand up. "Thank you. I really appreciate your taking the time to talk to me again. I'm sorry you're having to deal with all this. I'm sure it's scary. Are you thinking about moving away?"

She shakes her head. "I can't."

"Well, we are working really hard to resolve all of this, and hopefully, very soon, you'll be able to feel safe," I tell her.

"Thank you," she says.

She walks me to the door, and I step out into the deepened darkness. Night comes fast this late in the year, and even in the short time I was in Lilith's house, the light has completely disappeared. When she closes the door behind me, there is nothing but the faint glow of her porch light and the moon overhead to guide me along. Now, there's only darkness.

I take out my phone and turn on the flashlight, so I have some illumination at my feet to help me through the woods.

There is a creepy feeling at the back of my neck as I walk toward the cornfield. Of eyes on me. Like somebody's watching.

I have a feeling if I look over my shoulder right now, I will see Lilith's face in the window. She said almost nothing. And yet so much.

Rather than walking to the corn maze, I cross through the cornfield, say goodnight to the officers who had relieved the ones from before and taken their place protecting the investigation, and get in my car. The drive to the corn maze only takes a couple of minutes down the narrow dirt road. It was only a couple of months ago that Dean and I walked through the rows of corn and saw the beginnings of the maze growing up in the late summer heat.

Now it's fully grown and surrounded by black fabric to create boundaries and keep people in. Any other year that would just be to elevate the fear. There was already a certain level of unease and fright that comes from being in a maze at night.

Add a barrier that prevents walking through the edge to escape, and the feeling of being chased, and it can quickly turn into terror. But that's why people come. They want the rush of adrenaline. They want the brush with danger their lives never offer them.

They know in the end they'll find their way out.

But the fabric has a more ominous feeling after the events of the last few months. It's not just there to create a more frightening atmosphere or keep people from cheating and leaving the maze through the back or one of the sides. It's there to control their movements and stop anyone from trying to creep to the cornfield.

There's something about the intrigue of death that makes people feel the need to prove themselves. I'll never understand that. There's nothing inherently frightening about a grave or even a body. It's what happened to it, why it exists, that can be chilling. Yet people still want to do things like sit in a grave or touch bones, thinking it gives them some sort of credibility.

It's the damage they can do, the disrespect they show, that causes a problem. They seem to forget these were once people. That should never be forgotten.

In my years in this line of work, I have learned to think of a body as nothing more than a body. I distance myself for as long as I need to in order to investigate and find out what happened. But after that, their humanity returns. I never lose sight of their lives. And what they've left behind.

CHAPTER SIXTEEN

I get to the maze, but there's no one around. The screams and laughter have stopped, and there are only a couple of cars parked toward the back corners of the parking area.

"Dean?" I call, walking up to the entrance.

I hear voices in the distance. It sounds like someone is inside the maze, but they don't sound as happy about it as the other people did. I take out my phone and call Dean, but he doesn't answer. The only choice I have is to go in and find him.

I go into the corn maze, trying to follow the voices echoing around the sharp corners. I turn left, then right, left again, then come smack into a dead end. I curse under my breath, heading back to retrace my steps, then take a left where I had previously taken a right. One of the scare actors lunges out and screams, but I just brush by him.

"Not right now," I tell him, holding up my badge.

The man stops awkwardly, not sure what to do, but I keep my ears perked for familiar voices. I can just make out Dean speaking to someone else, but it doesn't sound like Xavier. Whatever he is saying is rather animated, and I pick up my steps to reach them a bit faster, taking a right, a left, two more rights, getting stuck twice more in dead ends, running past a few more actors, and then finally coming out towards the end of the maze. When I get there, my heart sinks.

It's only Dean and the man running the maze. Xavier is gone.

"Where is he?" I ask, not bothering with introducing myself or other niceties.

"I don't know," Dean begins, shooting a look over at the heavyset man beside him. The man, whose nametag reads "Carl", looks surly and upset. "One of the scare actors jumped out at him, and he took off. This guy grabbed me as I chased him to tell me they are closing and to get out."

"We are closed. Your friend will find a way out," Carl says.

"The hell he will," I say cutting him off. "He's not... he's lost. Trust me. He is lost, and he will stay lost if we don't go get him."

"Yeah, well, one of the actors in the maze will guide him out," Carl grumbles and then picks up his walkie. "Code orange. We have one loose. Adult. Guide him out and close up," he said into the ancient-looking walkie-talkie.

There is a moment of silence as we wait for a response. Carl pulls the walkie up to his ear and then turns the knob a few times.

"Shit," he mutters.

"Shit what?" Dean asks.

"Battery must be dead," Carl says. "Seriously, folks, the best thing is for you to go outside and holler for him to find one of the actors and make his way out. I'll go get another battery for this thing up at the house."

With that, he walks away from us, and I turn to look at Dean. I shake my head.

"I'm going in after him," I say.

"Me too," Dean nods. "We should probably split up to cover more ground."

"Famous last words," I mutter. "Didn't you suggest that last time?"

"I feel more for the scare actors than Xavier, honestly. Who knows what they will think when he starts telling them all about whatever is on his mind."

We reach the first fork quickly. I nod to the fork closest to me. "I'll head this way. If you find him, shout really loud."

"Will do," Dean replies. "Keep your eyes open. I don't think all the actors are gone yet. Don't break anyone's arm off, will you?"

I grin a little and take off down the path. Dean's footsteps fade away, and suddenly, I am alone in the darkening corn. I mentally kick myself for not stopping and getting Xavier a cell phone or GPS or something before bringing him here. Not that I had any reason to predict he'd do something like this.

As I make my way around a corner, the hair on the back of my neck stands up. I blew through this whole maze earlier, but that was before I had to stay and linger in the darkness before I had to take note of every sound, every flash of movement.

Which, unfortunately, makes me a prime target. I prepare myself for the inevitable jump scare. At some point, someone is going to jump out and wave a plastic knife or something at me. I have to remind myself they're just teenagers and to not punch one of them in the jaw.

I make it a few stalks down before it finally happens. A kid, a good couple of inches shorter than me, jumps out a few feet in front of me, cloaked all in black, with a goofy rubber mask on. He waves a plastic knife at me, swiping close to the stalks rather than at me, and then runs off through the stalks on the other side.

My heart rate jumps a little, and I scold myself. I am an FBI agent who has seen more than my fair share of horrific violence, death, and destruction. There is no reason to be afraid when a sixteen-year-old in a cheap costume yells 'boo' in a corn maze. Despite the aggravation at myself, I try to enjoy the spirit of it as I push further into the corn.

A few more actors jump out, but I usually see them coming. Their hiding places are repetitive and obvious to anyone who has a sense of where danger might lie. Once or twice, I think I can hear Dean in the distance calling out for Xavier, but even with both of us calling out, he never responds.

I make the decision that the next scare actor who pops out at me will get explicit instructions from me as to what I need, and maybe a gentle reminder of my job title. The implicit threat of an FBI agent might be enough to end the charade once and for all.

I find myself deep in the corn, in a place that almost seems as if it's no longer part of the maze. As if whoever designed it figured no one would actually end up here. The darkness is already fully set in, and the string lights hanging among the stalks are far away, pitching me into near blackness. This area is still and silent, and I can barely see a few feet in front of me.

A rustling in the bushes behind me is immediately followed by a body running full force into me. I nearly grab it and toss it to the ground out of instinct, my brain stopping me mere seconds before my hands are full of their shirt and my hip thrusting out to throw them to the ground. I want to do it anyway to teach the kid that the 'no touching' rule is important for just this reason, but in a lucky flash of light, I catch a glimpse of familiar eyes.

"Xavier?" I ask, grabbing tight to the wiggling form in front of me. The eyes search my face and recognition dawns.

"Emma," he gasps with a hoarse whisper. "Emma, the boogaloos. The boogaloos are here."

"It's just actors, Xavier. For Halloween. For fun," I say, but he wiggles hard, and I lose my grip.

"Not the boys. The men. The reaper man," he says.

"Xavier, wait," I cry out in vain as his legs tangle with mine and I trip trying to catch him. He takes off and barrels through the stalks beside me. "Run, Emma! The reaper does not listen to the harvest!"

I scramble to my feet and take off after him, trying to keep him in my sight. As I crash into the next row, I can hear his feet, but it's too dark to see him. There's a fork in the road ahead, and the echo of his footsteps doesn't come clearly from either direction. I can't tell where he's gone.

Taking a few steps forward, I feel the prickling on the back of my neck again and turn. A shadow dips into the stalks behind me.

I shake my head, making a note to give the owner a talking to. It's one thing to scare people for Halloween fun and games, and another entirely to stalk them when they are clearly chasing someone who's distressed.

A crashing of more stalks to one side gives me a clue, and I take off after it. The lights in this area are non-existent, and I am quickly running out of any visual aids. I call out for Xavier, but he doesn't answer. I stop to listen for something, anything.

There—a rustle behind me. I whip my head around in that direction only to see the shadow dip back into the cornstalks. For a brief second, I catch the glint of light off metal high in the air. It looks like a scythe.

"Whoever you are, get out of here! The maze is closed. Tell the other actors to help me find my friend," I shout toward the place the shadow disappeared, but my only answer is silence.

"I don't have time for this," I mutter and take off toward the crashing sound.

As my feet pound the dirt, I hear steps behind me. Someone is running after me. Chasing me. I look back and see only the glimmer of light off metal again. Fear grips me, and I turn up the speed. I call out for Xavier. For Dean. There is no answer.

I chance a look over my shoulder and see nothing, and then turn back to the direction I am running. Suddenly, a searing pain rips through my arm, and I cry out and tumble forward.

I hit the ground hard and roll, catching only a glimpse of a hooded man, the scythe, dripping with my blood, barely visible above the stalks as he dives back in.

CHAPTER SEVENTEEN

"What the hell?" I cry out as I clamp one hand down over the wound.

I get to my feet and take back off, rounding a corner in the direction the hooded man went and nearly run face-first into Dean.

"Jesus," he exclaims as we grab each other, so we don't body check each other to the ground. "I heard you scream. Are you okay?"

"One of these sons of bitches cut me!" I say, realizing I am yelling. "It was a real scythe. The idiot had a real scythe!"

"What?" Dean stammers, completely confused.

"It doesn't matter. I saw Xavier. He was going this way," I say, chancing one last look down the direction the blade disappeared. Everything that way is silent and still.

"We need to get you bandaged," Dean says.

"We need to find Xavier," I tell him forcefully. "There's someone running around in this maze with a real weapon. I don't think it's part of the show."

Dean's face hardens, and he nods.

We take off in the direction I saw Xavier running. We round a corner and come to a skidding stop. Xavier is lying on the ground, in the middle of another fork.

"Xavier!"

I rush toward him and drop to my knees on the ground beside him.

"What's going on?" Xavier asks as I yank open his jacket looking for wounds. "I'm fine."

"What?" I ask. "You're not hurt?"

"No," he says, a confused, almost sour look on his face. "Emma, look," he says. I try to follow his gaze. He points up, into the inky black sky, littered with distant white lights. "Find the belt. It can guide you."

"Orion's belt," Dean says. "He's looking at the stars."

"That's right," I say, setting my forehead onto his chest for a moment to catch my breath and compose myself. "You can find your way out by the stars, Xavier."

As I look up again, he grins at me, and I help him to his feet.

"I know how to get out from here," Dean says. "Let's just stay together, okay?"

"I am—I am never splitting up with you again, Dean," I manage a chuckle. The chase left me exhausted.

Xavier nods, and we begin to jog, following Dean. When we get into the light, Xavier grabs me by the arm and pulls me to him.

"Dean," he calls out, alarmed. "Dean, she's hurt!"

"I know. We need to get her bandaged up," Dean says, jogging back to us. "Oh."

"Oh? Oh what?" I ask, still struggling to get out a full breath.

"That is a *lot* of blood," Xavier says, his voice lucid and in control. "You need to get out of here right now. To help."

I look down at my arm for the first time since I ran into Dean. Blood soaks my shirt, and my hand is a mask of red. As soon as I notice it, I realize I am getting light-headed from blood loss.

"The exit is just down here," Dean says. "Let's go."

We move quickly, and a few turns later, we exit the corn maze into the empty field, and the bright lights of the entranceway to the maze.

We burst out of the maze and run over to a pile of hay bales stacked to one side. Dean turns me around and sits me down, pulling off my jacket so he can better see the cut on my arm.

"What the hell is going on?" Carl demands, stalking toward us. "I told you we're closed, and you went in there to have your own private tour."

"Call the police," Dean says.

"You know, I should," he sneers.

Dean stands up and takes a sharp step toward him, getting to within only a couple of inches of his face.

"Now," he growls. "Call the police and get an ambulance."

"An ambulance?" he asks, looking around Dean. The color drains from his face when he sees my arm. "What happened?"

"There's a man in the maze with a scythe," I tell him. "A reaper."

Carl shakes his head. "No. We don't have any actors dressed as a reaper with a scythe."

"I didn't say there was an actor," I say. "It's real. The scythe. He attacked me with it."

He holds up his hands like he's trying to prove his innocence, shaking his head, and backing up from me.

"I don't know what's going on here, but there's nobody in that maze but some teenage kids earning a couple of bucks an hour to jump out and scare people," he says.

"Look," Dean says through gritted teeth. "I don't care what you think. You have a wounded FBI agent here, and I suggest you stop trying to cover your ass and do what I say. Call the police and an ambulance. Now."

Dean comes back to me and looks at my arm. He stands up and walks over to a scarecrow a couple of feet away. Pulling off its shirt, he tears the fabric into strips and wraps them tightly around my arm to stop the bleeding.

"Xavier," I say, my words very quiet to preserve my strength. "You told me you saw the reaper."

"Yes," he nods. "He was in the maze."

"Did you see his face?"

"No," he says.

"Did he come after you?"

"Yes," he says. "That's why I ran."

I nod and look at Dean. "That was no kid. Somebody knows Xavier is out, and we had access to the temple. They're trying to stop us. This was a warning."

"I'm sorry," Xavier says.

"There's no reason for you to be sorry," I tell him. "You didn't do this. Besides, did you have fun?"

He nods. "Yeah."

I smile at him through the pain. "Good. That's good."

"Emma, you doing okay?" Dean asks.

"Feeling light-headed," I say.

"They're going to be here soon," he tells me. "Just stay awake."

"I am," I nod. "I'll be okay."

"Talk to me," Dean says. "How did the conversation with Lilith go? Did she tell you anything else?"

"Not really," I say. "But she was very focused on making sure I know she's a widow."

"What do you mean?" he asks.

"She said it probably five times," I explain. "Every opportunity she could to wedge it into the conversation, she would mention that she was a widow on her own, or that she had been widowed. She really wanted to emphasize not just that she was a single woman living out here, but that her husband is dead."

"Why would she want to do that?" he asks.

"I don't know," I say.

My voice is getting softer. The fabric Dean wrapped around my arm is soaked through with blood. He adds another on top of it, tying it tighter to try to stop the bleeding. Xavier crouches down in front of me and takes both of my hands.

"You're on a roller coaster," he says.

"What?" I ask.

"You're on a roller coaster," he repeats. "It's that moment when you first get in and they put the restraints down. You know they're tight enough, but you push them anyway just to make sure. Even though you're excited and you can't wait to ride, there's that split-second of fear. You're worried and wonder if you can get out before they start the ride."

"But you never can," I say.

He shakes his head. "No. Because it starts too fast. It jumps ahead and turns the corner to start to head down the first stretch. You hit the bottom of the hill and start creeping up. The chain clicks. It pulls you. Building up your excitement. You know the more clicks you hear, the higher the hill. The bigger the drop. You get to the top and the train sits there for a second. Just a second. Lasts forever, but it's just a second. Then right when you think nothing is going to happen, you drop."

My hands tighten around Xavier's as I focus on the sound of his voice and drawing in each breath.

"The pressure of being drawn up the hill releases. As if there's no control anymore. You're just on the track, sailing around the corners and over the hills. There's wind in your face, and you're scared, but you know you're safe. The restraints have you. They won't let you go. You're having fun, and you scream. Everybody around you is scream-ing. Can you hear them?"

The sound sinks into my ears, and I feel a little rush of the thrill that comes from giving in to a ride like that. The screams keep getting louder, and after a few seconds, I realize they aren't screams. It's the sound of sirens.

I didn't realize my eyes were closed until I open them. Lights from the emergency vehicles flash over my face, and I look at Xavier. He smiles.

"You made it," he says, then leans toward me. "See? It works for you, too."

CHAPTER EIGHTEEN

"Well, damn, my imagination is a whole lot better than I thought it was," I note.

"Maybe if she claps her hands together really hard, she can make all the scarecrows come to life, too," Dean says sarcastically, pacing back and forth across the hospital room.

"All we're trying to say is there isn't any evidence of what you described," the officer in front of me says.

"No evidence?" I ask. "Is the eight-inch gash down my arm I just had to have stitched up like a quilt, not enough evidence for you?"

"I'm sorry, Miss Griffin, but we spoke to the manager," the officer, somebody I vaguely recognized as having seen at the police station, says.

"It's Agent Griffin," I correct him. "And we spoke with the manager, too. He already gave us the line that he doesn't have a reaper scare actor in the maze. Which is why we tried to explain to him this was not one of his scare actors. This was somebody who went into that maze with the intention of coming after Xavier and me. Probably Dean, too."

"But you're the only one who got hurt," the officer says.

"Lucky me," I say, my eyes narrowing to glare at him.

"I understand you're upset. But the point of those mazes is to frighten people and make them feel disoriented. It's entirely possible you went in, got confused, and got scared by the actors. You were running and maybe saw one of the props, and you thought it was a person who came after you."

"And this?" I ask, gesturing toward the bandage wrapped around the long stretch of stitches down my arm. "I just scared this into being, too?"

"No," the officer says. "But there is some barbed wire at the back of the maze. It was supposed to just be a display, but it somehow got moved and ended up partially overhanging the walkway. You probably didn't even notice that you ran into it because you were so afraid."

"You're telling me you think I went into a corn maze and was so delirious and out of my mind with terror that I conjured up the image of a man with a scythe, ran into barbed wire, and believed it was him attacking me? That's your working theory right now?"

"It's the only thing that makes sense," he shrugs.

"That makes sense?" Dean sputters.

"I'm sorry," he says. "If there was more that we could do for you, we would. But we had men go through that entire maze. There was nobody dressed the way you described. We found blood, but no weapons."

"On the barbed wire?" I ask.

"What do you mean?" he asks.

"Did you find blood on the barbed wire? This cut is bad enough for me to have bled all over the maze itself, so if you're so sure that it was the barbed wire that cut me, logic would have it there would be blood on the wire. Right?"

The officer doesn't answer, and I shake my head, but before any of us can say anything else, the doctor comes in the room.

"How are the stitches feeling?" he asks.

"Like stitches," I tell him. "So. Fantastic."

"If we hear anything else, we will be in touch," the officer says.

He and the officer who stood silent beside him the entire time they were in the room nod and make their way out. Dean rolls his eyes and paces back to the window.

"You look like you're feeling a bit better," the doctor says.

I nod. "I am. Thank you, doctor."

"Good. Getting some fluids and blood back in you is usually pretty effective. It's a good thing you stayed calm. If you had panicked and the blood was pumping out of you faster, it could have been much worse. The cut is deep and caused some significant damage. Nothing that's going to stop you from using your arm or anything but expect it to hurt for a good while."

"Can she go home now?" Dean asks.

"No," the doctor tells him. "I want to keep her for observation and to make sure those stitches are doing alright. She'll be more comfortable here. We'll keep the IV going and be able to give her something for the pain when she needs it. Right now, she needs some rest so her body can start healing."

I shake my head adamantly. "I can't stay in here. I have investigations I have to do."

"Then you're going to have to do them from here," he says. "That's not a minor cut, Emma. You lost a lot of blood, and who knows what could have been on that blade when it cut you. You just stay here and let us make sure you're healing."

"Can they at least bring me my computer? My case files?" I ask.

"They can," he says. "But it would be better if you just tried to relax."

"She doesn't know how to relax," Dean says. "I feel lucky she didn't try to sew herself up with the remnants of the scarecrow and just go back to work."

"As long as you stay in bed and your IV stays in place, you can do whatever you want," the doctor says. "But for right now, get some rest."

He walks out of the room, and Dean comes to the side of the bed.

"What do you want to do?"

"I don't think smuggling me out is an option," I comment.

"It is," Xavier says from where he's sitting on the couch at the side of the room. "I've seen it done. I can be complicated, though. I don't think your IV stand would go along with you very easily."

Dean stares at him for a few seconds, then slowly turns back to me. "We'll consider that plan B. We'll just keep it right there in our back pocket. Other than that? What do you want to do?"

"Well, it seems that I'm going to be stuck here at least for a little while. So, I'm going to use my time wisely, piecing together what happened. Start with Lilith Duprey. I want you to find out absolutely everything you can about her. Everything. Who she is, who she was before she moved to Salt Valley, why she was so concerned about emphasizing that she is a widow."

"You're sure she has something to do with this?" Dean asks.

"She mentioned the shed," I say.

"What?" Dean asks.

"The shed. The one that's by the cornfield. When we were talking about the field and everything that's happened in it, she insisted she doesn't know anything about it. That she never goes near that field because when she first moved there, they told her that the field wasn't part of the property, and she doesn't even know who owns it. She said everything past those trees is off-limits to her, so she never goes over there."

"Alright," Dean says. "That would make sense. If I happened to live on property near a field where they found a bunch of bodies, I probably wouldn't want to get anywhere near it, either."

"But she mentioned the shed. She said she never goes past the shed. You can't see that shed from her house. It's hidden by the trees. She would have had to have gone to that field at some point to even know it's there. It's not a smoking gun, but it's something. It's an inconsistency. And when we have this little to go on, I'm willing to latch onto an inconsistency."

"I'll go by the hotel and grab you some clothes and your toothbrush and stuff," Dean says.

"Thank you." They start out of the room, and I lean forward slightly. "Xavier?"

"Hmm?" he asks, coming back in and standing next to the bed.

"Thank you. For what you did out there."

"You're welcome. I love amusement parks. They make me happy."

"Really?" I ask. "You don't strike me as the amusement park type."

"There are always surprises in this world," he says with a smile. "Rest well, Emma."

I don't want to sleep. There's too much to do, too many questions to answer. Every time I close my eyes, the looming black figure with a scythe appears behind them. He could have killed me easily, but he didn't. Just like I told Dean, the attacks were a warning. Somebody was trying to scare me away from the investigation. The fact that he went after Xavier, too, means we're close.

Which means I'm not stopping.

CHAPTER NINETEEN

I must have fallen asleep at some point during the night because the next thing I know, I'm waking up to the feeling of somebody stroking the back of my hand. I open my eyes and see my father sitting on the chair next to my bed. Worry is etched across his face, and his eyes are rimmed with red.

"Dad?"

"Hey, honey," he says.

"What are you doing here?"

"Dean called me," he says. "They told me you were hurt. I came as soon as I could."

"I'm okay," I tell him, adjusting myself to sit upright. "Really. It's just a cut."

But even as I protest, a wince of pain in my shoulder slows my movement. He looks at the bandage wrapped around my arm and the IV still dripping fluids into my vein.

"That doesn't look like just a cut, Emma. And he told me what happened. You were attacked?" he asks.

"Yes. Not that the police are doing anything about it. They talked to the manager of the maze, and because he said he doesn't have anybody working for him that dresses like that, they say it had to be a figment of my imagination. According to them, I ran into barbed wire because I was too scared to know what was happening," I say.

"That's bullshit," my father sighs. He looks embarrassed. "I'm sorry."

"No," I say, shaking my head. "I think that about sums it up. But I really am fine. You didn't need to come all the way out here just to check on me."

"I will come anywhere I need to check on you. You might be an adult, but you will always be my baby. I missed ten years of checking on you and taking care of you when you were hurt or sick. I'm not missing it one more time. Besides, I just finished an investigation. I thought maybe I could help with what's going on here," he says.

"Maybe," I say. "But first I have to actually figure out what's going on. It's so confusing. Just when I think I've figured something out or I'm on the right path, a complete detour will happen, and I'm totally thrown off track again."

"That's happened before," he notes. "And you always get through it. Have you talked to Sam?"

"I called him last night. He wanted to come, but I stopped him. He's already taking so much time away from Sherwood, I don't want to cause him any more trouble," I say.

A sudden realization hits me, and I hang my head low.

Dad tilts his head to look at my face as I stare down at my lap.

"What's wrong?" he asks.

"I forgot to make his cinnamon rolls," I say.

"What?" he asks.

"When I was at home, I promised I would make him cinnamon rolls and put them in the freezer so he could have them when I wasn't there. Then I got the call from Creagan saying Xavier had gotten a hearing about a new trial, and he was securing a search warrant for the temple. I was so wrapped up, I completely forgot," I explain.

"It's just cinnamon rolls," Dad says. "I'm sure Sam is fine."

"He is," I nod. "And that's the problem. He's fine with it. He shouldn't be. Because it's not just cinnamon rolls. It's something I told him I would do for him; then, I brushed it aside because of work. I don't want to do that. I don't want to be that person. It's why I broke up with him in the first place."

"What do you mean?" he frowns.

The realization sinks in that my father wasn't around when Sam and I broke up. He didn't experience that with me.

"After you disappeared, Sam tried to be there for me. He was amazing. He always has been," I say.

"He has," Dad says. "I knew from the time you two were little that there was something special between you. When you started dating, I figured that was it. You two were going to be together forever."

"Exactly," I say. "He was absolutely everything to me. I couldn't imagine a single moment of my life without him, and that meant I couldn't think about anything else. I had never gotten over that I didn't know what happened to Mama. She was gone, and nobody was ever going to tell me what happened. There were so many stories, so many lies, and cover-ups."

"I'm sorry," he says, his lips pulled tight into a remorseful grimace. "I'm sorry I ever put you through that. I thought it was what was right, that it would help you."

"It didn't," I say. "It made me confused and anxious. It wasn't until I was an adult that I realized I believed completely conflicting things about her death. But when you disappeared, too, I knew I had to do something about it. I couldn't just keep studying art and thinking everything in the world was fine. Because it wasn't. And I wanted to change that. So, I decided to join the Bureau."

"I don't understand what that has to do with Sam."

"Before I went into the academy, I knew that I couldn't stay with him. It just wouldn't work. Because he was so perfect. Because we were so good with each other. All I wanted was to be in Sherwood and have a home with him. Which would mean I would never be able to concentrate on investigations. I would never be able to really throw myself into the career I decided I wanted. I never wanted to be a woman who chose her work first and forgot about the little things. And I never wanted to neglect my work and possibly ruin an investigation or let a bad guy go because I was too focused on home.

"I broke up with Sam, so we'd never get to a point in our relationship when something was suffering. I always believed it was going to be my work. That I wouldn't be able to concentrate, or that I wouldn't feel comfortable doing investigations or field work because I wouldn't want to get hurt. But now I realize I didn't put my career at risk to be with Sam. I'm putting being with Sam at risk. I can't do that," I say. "He doesn't deserve that."

"Emma, what he deserves is you. Sam loves you. He always has. So, you forgot to make him cinnamon rolls. There was a lot going on. He understands. His father was sheriff before him. He knows what it is to be a part of law enforcement," Dad says.

I shake my head slowly. "I just don't know. Every single fiber of my being wants to be with him. But I want him to be happy. I want him to be able to have the kind of life he imagined. What if I can't give that to him?"

The door opens, and Dean and Xavier come in chatting. They stop when Dean notices me brushing tears away from my cheeks.

"What's wrong?" he asks. "What happened?"

I shake my head and force a smile. "Nothing. I'm fine."

"Hey, son," Dad smiles, standing up and giving Dean first an awkward handshake, but then they pull each other into a hug.

"Hey, Uncle Ian," he says. "Good to see you."

"Good to see you, too."

"Dad, this is Xavier," I introduce. "Xavier, this is my father."

"Ian Griffin," Dad says, extending a hand toward Xavier.

Xavier hesitates and looks at Dad's hand. Dad's eyes slide over to me, and I shake my head subtly. Dad lets his hand drop and continues smiling at Xavier.

"We have answers for you," Xavier says to me.

I almost want to laugh. He can't take himself off the track he was already on. He wasn't expecting my father to be here, so he can't change the direction of his thoughts to interact with him before getting out what they came to tell me.

"Go for it," I say.

"It's about Lilith Duprey," Xavier says. "We did what you asked and looked into her. And we found out something she kept buried underground, even when you tried to dig it up. The shape is still correct, but the weight is all wrong. Something is missing from it."

"She wasn't telling you the whole truth. Her husband was murdered ten years ago," translates Dean.

"He was murdered?" I ask. "What happened?"

"Don't know," Dean says. "It's still unsolved. But ten years ago is right about when Lilith started renting out her house in Salt Valley."

"That's why she wanted me to know she was a widow," I say. "She emphasized that over and over. She wanted me to know about his murder. That's why she moved. He was probably killed in the old house, and she didn't want to live there anymore."

"That makes sense," Dean says. "It also explains why it changed renters several times. Not many people like the idea of living in a house where someone died."

"I wouldn't mind it," Xavier chimes in.

We look at him, and his eyes widen slightly as if he didn't realize he said that out loud.

"You wouldn't?" I raise an eyebrow.

He shrugs. "At least that way, I know the people who lived there before me don't miss it. And I have to get used to feeling that way, don't I?"

I swallow hard and nod.

"What else?" I finally ask, trying to shake the emotion out of my head.

"Well, her husband was murdered, and she moved out of the house. But a decade before his murder, he was embroiled in a scandal," Dean says.

"Embroiled, no less," I note.

"I think that's the proper term when it involves politicians," Xavier says.

"Her husband was a politician?" I ask.

"He was," Xavier nods. "One of those white knight types. Loved by all. Always smiling. Too big a smile."

"He's pretty much a folk hero," Dean says. "His name is still invoked to this day by the causes he championed."

"And we all know how accurate those depictions are," I comment. "But this one has a past. So, what happened? What was the scandal?"

"We're not sure," Dean says.

"What?" I ask.

"We weren't able to find all the details yet," he tells me. "But we know it involves a woman named Lindsey Granger."

"Who is that? Another politician?" I ask.

"Another mystery," Xavier says. "We can only see her shadow."

I rub my temples with my fingertips. "This is insane. We've got another person who is missing, Lilith going from glamorous politician's wife to Green Acres. And somehow, in all this, she ends up wrapped up with a cult."

"Not a cult," Dad corrects me quickly.

"What?" I ask.

"The Order of Prometheus isn't a cult. It's a secret society, a fraternal order. It's not the same thing," he says.

"How do you know about the Order of Prometheus?" I ask. "Did the CIA investigate it?"

I haven't even considered the possibility, but now that the thought has gone through my mind, I'm excited. If Dad has already investigated it, he might be able to give me more insight into it and help trap them.

"No," he says. "I haven't investigated it. I'm in it."

CHAPTER TWENTY

TEN YEARS AFTER DEATH...

She couldn't cry. The dead don't mourn. At least, not from their graves.

After ten years, she no longer had eyes to cry. The sockets in her skull would be forever empty, with only raindrops to pretend at tears.

But even if she could cry, even if she could mourn, would she?

Were there ever tears cried for her? Did he ever, even once, stop and wonder what was happening to her?

It wasn't easy now. His skull still had eyes, but they couldn't see anything. Hers closed before her face dropped into the puddle, in the seconds after her heart stopped and her brain flashed in an instant of vibrant, explosive life.

His stayed open. They locked on the black and white floor and the rivulets of blood that flowed along the narrow seams between the tiles. Each tiny hexagon was nestled down into that floor individually. The grout crisp and white. It was just slightly uneven, making the blood pool and dip until it formed brilliant scarlet shapes that led away from him toward the slice of sunlight coming through the curtains.

Maybe he saw that sunlight in those last flashes of brain activity. Or maybe he saw her.

Her before the dirt, before the rain, before the sheet, before the puddle. Her before the cloud-covered starlight and the angry words. Her when he still knew what she looked like.

No one would come to tell her that he was gone. No one would whisper the words to her grave and hope the water seeping through her could carry them up to where she might hear them. No one knew she was there. And it seemed no one ever would.

But maybe there was someone who knew. Someone who would never say it but could feel it.

CHAPTER TWENTY-ONE

"What do you mean you're in it?" My mouth is gaping open.

I have no idea how long it's been since my father announced he was a member of The Order Of Prometheus. The shock makes it feel as if it could have been hours. Hopefully, it was only a few seconds.

"I'm a member," he shrugs. "So was your grandfather and your great-grandfather."

I close my eyes, shaking my head. My brain feels as if it's rejecting the words, it just won't accept them and let them fully process so I can understand what he's saying.

"I don't understand," I say. "How could you be a member? I'd never even heard of it before I came here."

"As I said, Emma, it's a secret society. It's not something the members talk about. The men in my family have a tradition of joining. We join at eighteen," he says. He looks over at Dean. "J—your father was in it with me."

I feel as if I'm going to be sick. My stomach surges, and my throat tightens up. I look over at Dean. His face is like a stone.

"Who did you kill?" Xavier asks.

I have to give it to him. He's able to put a voice to things I can't claw out of the corners of my brain.

Dad looks at him with surprise.

"I didn't kill anybody," he says.

"I suppose that's what they all say," Xavier says. "That is the point, isn't it? To kill and make sure somebody else takes the blame for it?"

"No," Dad says. "I didn't kill anyone. I belong to a different chapter of The Order. That's what I've been trying to tell you. This chapter in Harlan isn't like the others. This chapter has gone rogue. But the problem is, the ties of brotherhood are tight. Loyalty runs deep. It'll be next to impossible to get people to talk."

"Even if they know something horrible is happening?" I ask.

"Most likely, they don't talk to other chapters about what they do. And if they do talk about it, it's to people they know or have the same mind. The Order operates in individual chapters, but we don't monitor or govern each other. Something poisoned this chapter and twisted it into something The Order doesn't stand for. But anything that happens is protected by secrets and oaths. Just like anything else that happens within The Order, they aren't going to talk about the murders. They've become ritual just like everything else. They're part of how these people operate, and they don't differentiate them from any other element of The Order."

"So, what you're telling me is I'm never going to be able to prove it. Every one of them is just going to back each other up, and I'm never going to be able to prove the truth," I say.

"Not necessarily," he replies. "It will be difficult. I'm not going to lie about that. You just have to find a way to prove it without relying on one of them to tell you."

My brain is so saturated with thoughts and questions, I barely even notice when the doctor comes in and asks everybody to step out so he can check my sutures. I expect him to discharge me so I can get back to work. Instead, he tells me exactly what he feared has happened.

"We tried to clean the cut as thoroughly as possible, but that doesn't always work. There are now signs of infection," he says.

"What does that mean?" I ask.

"Because of the size of the cut and the potential for the infection to get very serious, very quickly, you're going to have to stay here for another night so we can administer antibiotics."

"Can't I just fill them at the pharmacy?" I ask.

"It's not that easy," he says. "In order to effectively combat the infection and ensure it does not worsen into a very serious condition, the antibiotic needs to be administered through your IV. If you respond well, you'll be able to be discharged tomorrow afternoon."

He starts to leave, then hesitates. "While you're here, you really should try to relax. Your stress levels are extremely high. Getting some rest will help your body recover and recuperate."

I can't rest. Even after he leaves, I can't make my mind or my body fully relax. I'm awake late into the night and have only just drifted off to sleep when my room door opens.

I open my eyes just enough to see Xavier slip inside and walk over to the couch.

"Hey," I whisper.

"I'm sorry," he says. "I didn't mean to wake you up."

"It's fine," I say. "Are you here alone? Where's Dean?"

"He's down in the cafeteria," Xavier says. "I wanted to return the favor. You always came to see me. So now I'm coming to see you."

I pull myself up to sit a little straighter and manage a smile.

"I think it's a little different," I say.

He nods seriously. "You're right. It is. They never had me hooked up to anything."

I look over at the IV and the fluids still dripping down into my vein.

"That's true," I chuckle weakly.

He sits down on the couch and stares into the space in front of him. His hands are folded in his lap, and he doesn't move for several long seconds.

"Something on your mind?" I ask.

"When a farmer sows seeds, he does it the same way every time. He scatters grass seed for the fields to feed livestock or for wildflowers.

He builds mounds for pumpkins. He digs deep trenches for corn. Everything is done the same way. He doesn't suddenly start scattering pumpkins or digging trenches for wildflowers."

"Right," I say.

"Those bones in the cornfield were all treated the same. Except for Lakyn and the cage. But even she was left out on the ground. They were scattered."

"Yes."

"So, if that's the way that farmer sows his crops, he always scatters, why did he suddenly dig a trench?"

That's why he's staring into the distance. He's not here with me. Xavier is back in the cornfield, looking at the grave. He's fixated on it, drawn to it for some reason, and he can't let go.

"Maybe it's a different kind of crop?" I offer, trying to put my mind into the type of space where murders are treated differently depending on the purpose behind it, like Lakyn's versus Andrew's.

"Or a different farmer."

"What's bothering you, Xavier?" I ask.

He shakes his head. "I don't know. It just doesn't fit the puzzle. The grave is too far from the other bodies and too precise. Someone took the time to dig that grave, put a wrapped body into it, and cover it up. None of the others was treated that way."

He sinks into thought again, and the room goes silent. A few moments later, he looks over at me, his eyes clearer, almost as if I'm looking at a different person. "The judge went on vacation."

I blink. "The judge? Sterling Jennings?"

He nods. "Dean and I were going to talk to him to see if we could catch him in another lie about Mason Goldman. I had everything ready. The script, the camera, the lights. But then when we got there, our star player was… gone. On vacation."

I would have loved to have heard the types of questions that Xavier wanted to ask the judge. Even more than that, I would have liked to see how he would react to having to sit there and look at Xavier, knowing what he did. And knowing that Xavier knows.

Even someone as cold as Sterling Jennings would have to react to that.

"Do you know where he went?" I ask.

"No," he says. "His secretary just mentioned that he's gone."

"I don't like that," I say.

"Why?" he asks.

"I don't like not knowing where he is. Especially considering my father tried to order dinner last night and found out that Lorenzo Tarasco's restaurant is temporarily closed for vacation."

CHAPTER TWENTY-TWO

Dean comes in a few minutes later, and we explain the situation. With a promise to check in on the other men, Xavier and Dean leave. I call my nurse, and a bright, familiar smile shines at the doorway seconds later.

"Gloria," I frown. "What are you doing here?"

"I'm a nurse," she says. "I'm working. What are you doing here?"

"Apparently being a very bad patient," I tell her. "According to the doctor, I need to rest and not be so stressed."

"Why do I have a feeling you're going to ask me to go against those orders?" she asks, a hint of a smile in her voice.

"Because I'm going to ask you to go against those orders," I admit. "But only briefly. I promise it won't be anything crazy."

"What do you need?" she asks.

"I want to go up and see Millie. I just want to check in on her and see how she's doing. I promise I won't scream at anybody while I'm up there," I say.

She thinks about it for a few seconds. "Okay. According to your chart, you're only getting fluids right now. You're not due for another dose of antibiotics for another few hours. If I can trust that you don't have a getaway car waiting for you on the ground floor and you're just going to disappear, I'll put you in a wheelchair and let you go over there."

"The back half of my current outfit is missing, Gloria," I comment. "I don't think I'm much of a flight risk."

"Don't think I don't know that gorgeous man with the big muscles brought you clothes," she whispers conspiratorially.

For a few seconds, I don't know who she's talking about. Then it hits me.

"You mean Dean?" I ask.

"I don't care who he is. He's spectacular," she says. "Well done."

I make a face at her. "He's also my cousin. That's just weird. But I'll forgive you if you get this thing out of my arm and get me my wheelchair."

"So what you're saying is, he's available?"

"Can you please get me the wheelchair?"

"Oh, fine."

I flash a wide grin to encourage her along, and she shakes her head. Minutes later, I'm wheeling my way down the hallway to Millie's room. Gloria was nice enough to bring me a blanket to wrap around me as well, but I have every intention of going back to the room and putting some actual clothes on as soon as I'm done talking to Millie.

She's sitting up in her bed, looking perkier than the last time I saw her. Some of the pep drains out of her face when she sees me.

"Emma," she gasps. "What happened? Are you okay?"

"I'm fine. I'm surprised you didn't hear all the hospital gossip," I start. "Is that a thing? That's a thing, right? Hospital gossip. People talking about each other and their ailments?"

"You would have to ask somebody else," Millie shrugs. "I'm not exactly the gossip type."

"That's true," I nod. "You're not. But, in the interest of talking about people, I hear your big brother went on vacation this morning. That must be nice. Does he travel a lot? Go to the same place every year?"

She looks at me strangely. "Which brother?"

"Sterling," I tell her. "I figured there might be somewhere he likes to go whenever he decides to take a break from all the stress in his career and everything. Maybe a beach house? A mountain lodge? Skiing?"

I'm trying to sound as casual and breezy as I can, but I'm afraid it's coming across as faintly maniacal. Millie looks worried as she shakes her head.

"No," she says. "Not that I know of. He isn't exactly the vacationing type. He prefers to be buried in work all the time."

An interesting turn of phrase there, I think to myself.

"So, you don't have a family vacation house or anything? When I was growing up, we used to go to Florida a lot. I really love it there. It's still probably my favorite place in the world other than Sherwood."

I lean a little closer. "And sometimes I think I might actually like it more than Sherwood. But don't tell Sherwood that. It would upset it. Oh, no. I've been spending too much time with Xavier."

"Emma, what's going on?" Millie asks, breaking me out of my brief existential spiral.

"I just wanted to come by and check on you and see if you're feeling better. How your recovery is going," I say.

"And to ask me about my brother's vacation?" she asks.

I let out a sigh.

"I guess I'm not good at gossip, either."

"No, you're not. Why are you so fixated on his going away for a few days?" she asks.

"Why are you?" I counter. "I can see it all over your face. Don't act as if nobody knows where he is."

She draws in a breath and holds it for a second, seeming to hope a few extra seconds will somehow soften her words.

"I don't know where he is, Emma. I don't know where he would have gone. I know you think he did something horrible..."

"I *know* he did something horrible, Millie. A lot of horrible things," I say.

"But you can't prove it," she says.

"I can if someone helps me," I say. "Someone who knows him better than I do."

"I can't help you, Emma," she says sadly, for what must be the ten millionth time in all these conversations. "I just can't."

"Emma, if you get any more visitors, we're going to have to put a turnstile up at your room door," Gloria calls over from the doorway, making me turn and look over my shoulder at her.

"I have another visitor?" I frown.

"Yep," she says. "Want me to wheel you back over there?"

"No, I think I can do it."

"Your arm is not going to be very happy with all this exertion," she points out. "Don't you want your sutures to heal so you can eventually get out of here?"

"It's that 'eventually' you threw in there that brings it all home," I mutter with a roll of my eyes.

"Come on," Gloria smiles. "Enjoy the ride."

"You could probably say 'wheeeeeee' in the hallway while she's going, and she wouldn't be able to do anything about it," Millie cuts in.

Gloria points a warning finger at her. "Don't you go giving her ideas. You haven't been any trouble since you got here, so don't start now on account of Emma. You're getting out of here soon."

The news that she won't have to stay in the hospital for much longer should make Millie happy. Instead, I notice her face fall. She swallows and turns away to look out the window.

That stays with me as Gloria takes hold of the wheelchair handles and steers me back toward my room.

"Wheee," I say softly as we turn the corner.

She laughs and shakes her head. "None of that, now. Be a good role model."

"For who?" I ask. "The other adults recovering in the hospital?"

We get to my room, and she pushes me inside.

"You two, be nice. I don't want to have to come and break anything else up between you," she says.

I don't need any explanation for why she would say that. I can already see it. Sitting in the chair next to my bed, her eyes sideways, trying to read as much of the case notes piled on my side table as she can, is Lydia.

"What are you doing here?" I narrow my eyes in frustration.

"Emma," Gloria says. "Play nice."

"Hi, Lydia," I say. The nurse walks out of the room and closes the door. "What are you doing here?"

"I heard you got hurt," Lydia says. "What happened?"

"I got hurt," I tell her, climbing out of my wheelchair and getting into bed.

"Were you at the corn maze?" she asks. "I heard there was a lot of commotion up there the other night, and somebody got taken away in an ambulance. Was it you? And if it was, were you there because you were talking to Lilith Duprey?"

"Lydia, I tried to tell you. You are not part of this investigation," I say.

"Hear me out," she holds out a hand to stop me. "I know you've been asking around about her. You've gone and spoken to her a couple of times. There's something about her that interests you, and I think I have more information about her that you might like to hear. It could be helpful."

"Fine," I sigh, figuring any information she might be able to give me could be useful. "What have you got?"

Lydia grins and reaches into the bag at her feet to pull out a manila envelope. She hands it to me.

"She moved to Salt Valley twenty years ago. Ten years later, she moved to the farm," she says.

"I know," I nod. "When her husband was murdered."

"Yes," she says. "But do you know why she moved to Salt Valley?"

"Some sort of political scandal," I say. "I don't know the details."

"I do," she says.

I'm instantly intrigued, but I don't want to encourage her too much, so I give a nod. "Go ahead."

"Twenty years ago, Lilith's husband, Michael Duprey, was fairly early in his political career. He had already served a few years, was building up his name. But then rumors started swirling around that he was involved with a woman named Lindsey Granger."

"Who is she?"

"An intern," Lydia says.

"Of course she was," I say.

"Exactly. So, they denied it. He denied and denied and denied. She would never make a public statement. They were never seen in public together or photographed after the rumors started. But there were still people talking. Then, it stopped."

"Why did it stop?" I ask.

"Because she suddenly was just... gone."

"Gone? What happened to her?"

"That's the big question," Lydia tells me. "Nobody's really sure. She was seen going to a hotel, then nothing. People came up with all sorts of explanations, but nothing ever panned out. Michael, Lilith, and his daughter from a previous marriage, Rachel, put up a major united front. All of a sudden, they were this perfect, happy family. But here's the thing. Rachel was seen far more often than Lilith, and it was well known that the two of them didn't get along."

"So, he was using his little girl as a political bargaining chip. That happens," I comment.

"She wasn't a little girl," Lydia says. "Michael was much older than Lilith, and Rachel was already in college by the time all this was going on. She was well on her way to a political career herself. She stepped right into the role of campaigning for her father. She was his face of the youth. And when all the rumors were going around, she was extremely outspoken supporting him. That was the one time she and Lilith seemed to come together. Rachel seemed to take massive offense that anyone would think that her father would have an affair, first off, and second, that he would do anything to hurt a woman. She was determined to prove Lindsey was fine, and the affair never happened."

"Did she?"

"Not exactly. There were some sightings of Lindsey after that, but she never came back to Virginia to tell her side of the story. After that, most people started believing Rachel's story that Lindsey had tried to blackmail her father, and it didn't work because he was above reproach. Then when she realized that her grift had failed, Lindsey left in shame to start a new life. Since then, Michael skyrocketed in his political career, became an activist and advocate, and built a nice extra stream of income with motivational speaking and self-help seminars."

"Until he was murdered," I point out.

"Yes, that kind of put a damper on things. But thanks to Rachel's indomitable spirit, he might just be more popular now than he was even when he was alive. From what I've heard, the two women haven't spoken since his death, with both of them saying the other was responsible for all kinds of different reasons. Rachel inherited the majority of his estate, and they went their separate ways."

"If Lilith inherited anything, where did it go?" I ask. "She lives in that tiny cabin and doesn't seem to have much to her name."

"No idea," Lydia says. "For some reason, all that money is just missing." She leans back and smiles. "So, what do you think?"

"What do you mean, what do I think?"

"Did I prove I'm a good enough investigator? Can I help?" she asks, her face lit up with hope.

I tilt my head this way and that, considering it, but let out a sigh. More for appearances than anything else.

"You aren't an investigator, Lydia," I tell her. "You run an online sleuth website. A database of cold cases. You don't have the skills or the training to actually investigate something that's big and potentially dangerous. You could get hurt. You could compromise the work that's already been done. I really appreciate it that you found these things out, but I need you to just stay out of my way."

The smile fades from her face.

"Fine," she says. "I'll back off." She scoops her bag off the floor and storms toward the door. She stops just before walking out and turns to face me.

"But one day, Emma, you're going to have to forgive me for what happened to Greg. I might be convenient, but I'm not the one you should be blaming."

CHAPTER TWENTY-THREE

Lydia's words hang over me, haunting me long after she leaves. But I can't think about that right now. I don't have time to think about that right now. There are so many other things I have to figure out.

The details she gave me about Lilith and her past tumble around in my mind. It seems as if they're trying to fall into place. They're trying to make sense. I'm just not there yet.

Opening the folder Lydia gave me, I read through all the information again. She's included notes about everything she told me, as well as printouts from Rachel Duprey's website. The contact page has a picture of her. It's the quintessential image of a young woman in politics. Three-quarter profile, arms crossed at her waist. Slim navy pinstripes with a royal blue shirt underneath. Dark red hair swept up in a chignon shows off a long neck with a single delicate gold chain that drops a pendant right between her collar bones.

Her makeup is pristine and understated. The smile on her lips somewhere between reassuring and smug. I flip through the rest of the pages and find more images of her. These are less manufactured. They show her at various charity events and volunteer occasions. In some of them, her shirt is emblazoned with her father's name.

This is a woman who was deeply affected by her father's death and has carried him with her since then. I can understand that. I connect with her in that way, and it makes me want to know more about her. She was extremely young to be so involved in her father's political career, but it's obvious she burrowed her way in as soon as she could and never let go.

Maybe there's more she can tell me. An insight the interviewers weren't able to pick up on. Understanding what happened to Michael Duprey and his career is a starting place to understand how Lilith toppled so far.

Grabbing my phone from the night table, I call the private number Lydia scrawled across the top of the contact page printout. I don't know how she got it. I don't even know if I want to know how she got it. But before the third ring, Rachel answers.

"Hello?"

"Hi, is this Rachel Duprey?" I ask.

There's a pause before she answers.

"Yes, this is Rachel Duprey. How did you get this number?"

"Hi, Rachel, this is Emma Griffin," I say.

There's a brief pause on the other end of the line.

"I'm sorry, have we met?" she asks.

"No," I say. "We haven't."

"Any requests for appearances or business propositions that should be made through the foundation's direct line, not my personal line," she says. "Thank you."

"Wait," I say. "I'm not calling for a business proposition or request for an appearance. I'm actually with the FBI. I'm Agent Emma Griffin."

"Oh," she says. "What can I do for you, Agent Griffin?"

"I am looking into a series of events, and they seem to have a tie to your father," I say.

"My father?" she asks. "What could it have to do with my father?"

"I'm actually not entirely sure at this moment," I tell her. "We're still pretty early in the investigation. Which is why I'm calling you. I wanted to get your personal perspective and insights into the situation with Lindsey Granger."

"I'm going to stop you right there," she says. "There was no situation with Lindsey Granger. That was blown up by the media and turned into a smear campaign that dramatically affected my father's personal and professional life. He never fully recovered from the serious damage that was done with those rumors. They were baseless and indefensible."

"So, there was no relationship there?" I ask.

"Absolutely not," she says. "She was an intern who worked in the same building as my father. They may have walked past each other in the morning or stood in line for coffee a couple of times. It didn't go any further than that."

"Several sources say he was familiar enough with her to know her name and to be concerned about her when she seemed to disappear," I say.

"He knew her name because she was another human being," Rachel replies. "That was the type of man my father was. He cared about people. All people. It didn't matter to him what their job was or where they came from. If there was a human being in his vicinity, he was going to anything he could to help him or her. She worked in his building, so he learned her name. If he walked past her, he would say hello to her. And of course, he was concerned. Everybody was. But to speak to your choice of language, Lindsey Granger did not 'disappear'. She left town because she was humiliated after attempting to destroy the life of an honest, loving, and honorable man who refused her advances, then would not back down when she attempted to blackmail him."

"How would she blackmail him if nothing ever happened between them?" I ask.

"You work for the FBI, Agent Griffin?" she asks.

"Yes," I say. "For a number of years."

"Then surely you're familiar with lying and faking evidence. My father would never do the things that woman said he did. She did the best thing she possibly could by leaving and never showing her face around here again. It gave us all time to heal and move past her. That's what we've done, Miss Griffin. We've moved on. That was a long time ago, and I don't appreciate my father's name being dragged through the mud yet again. I won't speak about this again," she says.

"Then will you talk to me about his death?" I ask.

"Good day, Agent Griffin."

She hangs up, and I pull the phone down to stare at it.

"Well, that didn't go exactly as I planned," I mutter to myself.

The interaction was harsh and intense. I can understand that. This is a woman who has been through a lot, and it all happened in the spotlight. I still get protective and defensive when people talk about my mother and her murder. Rachel probably just wants to put the entire situation with Lindsey Granger in the past and never have to think about it again.

I'm certain she never wants to think about her father's murder again.

But I can't accommodate her just yet. I'm not convinced this is over.

The next morning, I start my day with two fantastic pieces of news. I'm on the phone with Sam as he tells me he's coming in later that afternoon, just as, when the doctor appears at my door with a stack of papers in his hand on a smile on his face.

"Hey, babe," I tell Sam. "I've got to go. The doctor is here with papers, and either he needs me to start signing away pieces of my body for experimentation, or he's going to discharge me."

"Make sure he contacts me first," he jokes. "I have dibs on a few of those parts."

"I'll see you soon. Love you."

I hang up and look at the doctor with hope.

"So, we thought we would start from the bottom and work our way up. The first thing we're going to do is amputate your feet. Actually, we'll probably start with your toes. Maximum surface area and all," he starts, barely suppressing his smile.

"Alright," I say, "but I have to warn you, a couple of those toes have been broken a few times, so they might not be the most responsive when it comes time to reanimate them."

The doctor laughs and comes to my bedside with my discharge papers.

"Your release papers," he says. "I've included aftercare instructions for your cut, as well as some lifestyle recommendations to keep your health up. There's a prescription for painkillers and antibiotics. You'll only need the antibiotics for a few days, with any luck. If you notice any symptoms that suggest the infection has come back..."

"I am to promptly remove my arm so I don't end up here again," I say.

"Or call the hotline and speak with one of the nurses," he replies. "It's going to be tender for a little while. You might have trouble lifting heavy objects, and your full range of motion might be compromised until it heals. You're going to want to keep exercising it, so you don't end up overworking the other or possibly reducing the strength in your injured arm."

"Thank you, doctor," I tell him. "I appreciate it."

"Any time," he nods.

I give him a look as I climb out of bed. "You know that's really not the best phrase to use when your job is stitching people back up and preventing them from dying of infections."

He thinks about that for a second. "Duly noted." With a wave, he walks out of the room and closes the door behind him.

I've been holding out on one outfit Dean brought me for this particular occasion, and I smile as I slip into it. Finally, I feel like a regular person again. Not like a patient, with people walking on eggshells around me. But a real person. It only takes me a couple of more minutes to gather everything, brush my teeth, and walk out of my room.

"You sure do whine a lot," Dean comments as soon as I step into the hallway.

"I do not whine," I protest, heading for the elevator. "What are you doing here?"

"I came to get you. You didn't drive yourself to the hospital, remember?"

"Oh, yeah," I say. "Well, thank you."

"You do whine," he says.

"I do *not*," I repeat, pushing the elevator button

"At the very least, you are a terrible patient."

"I don't like being in the hospital. I feel all cooped up and can't do anything," I say. "And people always treat me as if I'm some fragile little baby bird. I'm fine."

"Two days, Emma. You were in the hospital for two days. I was in longer when I ate that gas station sushi."

"Why would you eat gas station sushi?" I ask.

"The point is, it might have done you some good to actually take the doctor's advice and chill out a little bit while you were here. You've got the rest of us out here. We've got your back," he says.

"Thank you," I tell him. "I'm just really bad at hospitals. I don't have a lot of great memories revolving around hospitals."

"Martin is dead. He can't put you in a morgue drawer again. And even if somebody tried, I would be there to get you out again," Dean says.

"That's very sweet of you," I tell him.

"What are cousins for, if not to rescue you from near-death experiences?"

"Picnics and barbecues?" I offer. "Awkward Christmas pictures? Complaining about other relatives at Thanksgiving?"

"Good options," he grins. "We'll try all of them out. But for now, where am I taking you?"

"Have you and Xavier been staying at his house?" I asked.

"Yeah," he says. "And you should see this thing. It's insane. It's like Inspector Gadget designed it in cooperation with Martha Stewart."

"So, there's a kitchen?"

"Yes, Emma, there's a kitchen."

"Good. Let's go there," I say.

CHAPTER TWENTY-FOUR

"Not that I don't appreciate the smell of cinnamon rolls," Dean starts, "but why are you making them right after getting out of the hospital?"

"I don't care why she's making them; they're delicious," Xavier says, unraveling another one from my last batch into his mouth.

The thought flashes through my mind, and I wonder what the cinnamon rolls would say about him. It makes me smile to myself. I might have been around Xavier too much, but I can't say I hate the way he's changed my thoughts. Most of the time.

"Some of them are for Sam," I say. "I was supposed to make them for him before I left home, but I didn't. And he's coming here today, so I want to have them waiting for him. Unfortunately, the hotel I have been calling home does not have an oven. So, thank you, Xavier, for lending me yours."

He grins through a mouthful of cinnamon, dough, and cream cheese frosting.

"I think it's enjoying it. It's been a long time since anything was baked in here. And I never made cinnamon rolls."

"Well, it's rising to the occasion beautifully," I smile.

"Why are you still in the hotel?" Dean asks. "You have plenty of money. You could just rent a house for as long as you're going to be here in Harlan."

Just the suggestion makes me swallow hard and shake my head, but I can't come up with the exact words to answer him.

"Because this isn't where she wants her home to be," Xavier says.

"What?" Dean asks.

"Your surroundings become your identity. They are your reality. You can always hope for something different or dream that you're somewhere else. But you are where you are. There's never a guarantee you'll be anywhere else. If Emma rented a house here, that would be like saying this was her home now. That this is where she belongs. She can't do that. This isn't where she wants to tie her soul," Xavier says.

He hands me the now empty tray, and I start another batch of rolls in the silence his words left in their wake.

I'm standing in the middle of the hotel room with a plate piled high with cinnamon rolls when Sam comes in two hours later. He looks at them, takes the plate out of my hands to set aside on the desk, then scoops me into his arms and holds me close.

By lunch the next day, the cinnamon rolls are gone, and so is any of the relaxation I might have gotten from my stay in the hospital. Sam went out to grab us something to eat, and when he comes back, I'm sitting at the desk with my elbows propped on it, my fingers clenched in my hair as I stare at the papers in front of me. Dean is flat on his face on one of the beds, and Xavier is draped sideways across the other, his head hanging upside down from the side.

"Well, this looks like an optimistic and energetic bunch," Sam remarks, coming in carrying a bag full of white styrofoam containers from the sandwich shop down the street.

"We still can't find him," I tell him.

Sam sets the bag on the table and shrugs out of his jacket, draping it on the chair.

"Jennings?" he asks.

"Yes." I say releasing my hair and dropping my head back for a second, then turning to look at him. "We have talked to everybody we can think of. Travel agents. The other judges. I just got off the phone with his brother. Who is even more unpleasant than Sterling is, if you can believe it. And we are nowhere. Nobody knows where he is, and nobody thinks it's important for us to know where he is. It was as if Ron was finding joy in not being able to give us any information."

"Or choosing not to," Dean adds, his voice muffled by the bedspread.

I hold my hand up to underscore his point.

"Alright, everybody up," Sam says. "Did any of you hear from Detective White today?"

"No," I say.

"No," Dean says.

"I never hear from Detective White," Xavier says.

"Did any of you hear from Creagan today?"

"No," I say.

"No," Dean says.

"I also never hear from Creagan," Xavier says. "Emma," he grabs the bedspread beside him to give him leverage that he can pull his head up and look at me. "I need a cell phone."

"Yes, you do," I say. "We'll add that to the list."

"For today, that list is taking a half-day," Sam says.

"What do you mean?" I frown.

"We're going to eat lunch, then we're going to go do something fun," he says. "No more moping or investigating."

"There's too much to do," I say.

"Which is exactly why we are going to do something fun."

"You do realize that kind of sounds counterintuitive, right?" I point out.

"Look, everything that needs to be done will still need to be done when you get back."

"Not sounding too optimistic right at this moment," I say.

"The point is, you've been pushing yourself into the ground. You're working too hard, and it's going to catch up with you. I know you,

Emma. I know you better than anybody. And you work at your fastest and strongest and best when you haven't put yourself through a blender."

"I think that probably applies to everybody," Xavier points out, his head upside down again.

"See?"

"No," Sam says. "Emma, listen to me. I know this is important to you. It's gotten under your skin, and it's driving you crazy. But remember, we've had talks about this. I need you to take a step back. Just for a little bit. This is all you can see right now, and I need you to see something else."

He was asking me to see him. My conversation with my father rises up into my chest, tightens my throat, and makes my eyes burn. I try to breathe, but the air won't move. All I can do is nod.

"What did you get for lunch?" I ask him

A smile comes to his lips, and he picks up the bag. Sam distributes the sandwiches and bags of chips he got, and we position ourselves around the room to eat.

"What did you have in mind for the fun thing of the afternoon?" Dean asks.

"Well, I was thinking we could go to the pumpkin patch," Sam says. "It's something Emma always used to love when she was younger."

Our eyes meet, and I smile, for a second, only seeing him.

***

Just getting to the pumpkin patch already makes me feel more relaxed. It brings back memories from my childhood. I used to spend hours choosing the perfect pumpkins to sit on the porch. As teenagers, Sam and I would pick a day to go together. It was a perfect excuse to walk through the rows of vines holding hands and stealing kisses in the autumn chill.

The parking area in front of the pumpkin patch butts up against a row of stacked hay bales that supports a hand-painted wooden arch over the entryway. We walk through it into a large area filled with already picked pumpkins and gourds on display. Xavier immediately goes over to a section of the pumpkins displayed on risers, surrounded by smaller hay bales, and begins examining them.

Sam watches him for a few seconds.

"How are the pumpkins feeling today, Xavier?" he calls over.

Xavier glances over his shoulder at him, then back at the pumpkins. He runs his hand over one of them.

"Pretty smooth," he says. Then runs his hand over a decorative, ridge-covered one beside him. "Except for this one. This one's pretty bumpy."

Sam looks at me, and I laugh as he shakes his head. "I'm never going to get him. Never. As soon as I think I am on the right track... I'm just not going to get it."

I throw my arms around his neck and kiss him. "You try. That's all that matters. Come on, let's get a hayride."

For the next two hours, I don't think about anything but the guys, the gorgeous weather, and the pumpkins. I won't let myself. It feels too good to see Dean and Xavier bonding as they climb through the vines together in search of the perfect, untouched pumpkin. Or to turn around and already be in Sam's arms, my face able to nuzzle right in the crook of his neck so I can smell his aftershave and feel his heartbeat.

When we've collected an impressive assortment of pumpkins and stacked them by the road to be picked up with the hayride, I realize Dean and Xavier haven't come back from their last excursion.

"Do you know where they went?" I ask Sam.

"Last I saw them, they were headed off into the far corner, determined they were going to find the Great Pumpkin," he chuckles.

"Descriptor or gourd deity?" I ask.

"I think, descriptor?" he offers. "I don't think this place is sincere enough for anything else. The one back home is much better."

I nod and make an acknowledging sound. Sherwood was always my favorite pumpkin patch. Over the years, I would go to ones all over, always moving from state to state. But none of them ever measured up to Sherwood.

Cupping my hand over my eyes, I look out over the field, trying to see them. The rumble of the tractor pulling the hay wagon gets louder in the distance, and a cloud of dust puffs up. I grab my phone to call Dean, but the reception won't grab hold.

The tractor stops in front of us, and the handful of other people browsing the field climb on. I walk up to the side of the tractor to talk to the driver.

"We have a couple of stragglers," I tell him. "These are our pumpkins right here. Do you mind coming back for us?"

"No problem," he says. "Load up the pumpkins, and I'll bring them to the front to wait for you."

"Thank you," I say. "I appreciate it."

I lean down to grab one of the biggest pumpkins, and pain tears through my arm. The pumpkin drops back down to the ground as I pull my hand away from it, pressing my palm to my bandage and hissing.

"You alright?" Sam asks.

"I'm fine," I say. "Just sore."

"You didn't tear out any of your stitches, did you?" he asks.

"No. It's fine."

"Good. Let me get the big ones. You get the others."

We manage to pile everything into the corner of the wagon, and the driver pulls off. Sam and I turn back around to look out over the field, then venture out to look for Dean and Xavier.

CHAPTER TWENTY-FIVE

"There they are," I point, after another twenty minutes of looking for Dean and Xavier.

"What are they doing?" Sam asks.

"I don't know. Looks like they're looking at something. Dean! Xavier!"

They turn toward the sound of my voice and wave at me.

"Come over here!" Xavier says. "Look what we found."

Sam and I exchange glances. There's something slightly disconcerting about that coming out of Xavier's mouth. He doesn't seem upset, so at least there's that. Sam takes my hand, and we make our way through the tangled, matted vines in this all-but forgotten section of the patch. This must be where they pick the pumpkins that go to the displays at the front of the patch near the parking area.

With the exception of a few mangled remnants that either got too ripe on the vine and had to be left behind or otherwise met their end, this section of the patch is devoid of the bright orange pumpkins dotting the rest of the field. Sam's foot gets stuck under some of the knotted vines, and he tries to use me to catch his balance.

There's a touch-and-go moment when we could either get back to our feet or end up stumbling over each other onto the ground. Dean and Xavier wait while we negotiate with gravity, but we eventually come out still standing. When we get to them, Dean gestures toward a small wooden sign sticking up out of the ground beside a narrow, dark path leading into the woods.

"Haunted trail," he reads in a theatrical voice, adding a couple of ghostly sound effects for good measure.

"What is it?" I ask.

"A haunted trail," Xavier says.

"Thank you."

"I'm assuming it's part of their Halloween attractions," Dean says. "We got turned around while we were in the patch and were trying to find our way back out."

"No stars," Xavier says.

Dean gestures toward him and nods. "But we figured the patch couldn't go on forever."

"Both for logical permanence of space reasons and because we could see the trees," Xavier adds.

"So, we headed this way thinking we'd probably find a path leading back up to the front of the patch."

"But we got stuck," Xavier says.

"But we found this," Dean says, holding his hands up dramatically to display the sign.

"Well, it is a path," Sam observes. "So you were in the right general sphere."

"Let's go down it," Xavier says. "I want to see what's down there."

"Can we just remember for a second what happened last time we decided to go through something haunted?" I ask.

"Come on, Emma," Dean says. "It's the middle of the afternoon. Bright daylight. I doubt anybody is even down there. It would just be interesting to see the sets. Remember, we're doing 'fun Halloween.'"

He does another gesture with his hands, sweeping them in circles to either side of his face like a magician talking about an illusion. I glance over at Sam. He makes the same gesture, and I know I'm outnumbered.

"Alright," I relent. "But if there is a reaper down there with a scythe and he takes out my other arm, I am going to be pissed."

I want to be joking, and part of me is, but there's another part of me that is glad my gun is tucked securely in my holster, and my knife is concealed under my shirt. That's Sam's doing. My gun is always enough to make me feel confident, but it's not enough for him.

Somebody can take your gun, he always tells me. Somebody can kick it out of your hand. Have something else. That's how I ended up with a specialized bra designed to hold a small knife against my rib cage. In all honesty, it sounded absolutely ridiculous when I first heard about it. But, to comfort Sam, I bought it. It was meant to be like the pumpkins up at the front of the patch, a display piece. But then I thought about it some more and realized it wasn't that terrible an idea for somebody in my line of work.

I haven't had reason to use it yet, but I'm glad it's there.

We start down the path, and it's not long before I'm confident Dean was right in his assessment. The path is wider once we get past the entrance into the trees. The deep ruts under our feet tell me this is actually used for a haunted hayride rather than a walking path.

To either side of the path, Halloween decorations and gory props create tableaus of various horrific scenes. They aren't as convincing in the daylight. Rubber and paint are pretty harmless when the sun is pouring down on them. But darkness and strobe lights can make almost anything seem scary. Throw in the sound of a chainsaw, and rubber and paint get disturbing real fast.

"Jeez," Dean remarks as we walk past a dilapidated cabin with what looks like a half-man half-pig butcher sitting on the front porch cradling a meat cleaver and human head. "This looks like we're strolling through Hannibal Lecter's Viewfinder."

"What's a Viewfinder?" Sam asks.

"You know," Dean says. "From when we were kids. That red thing. It looks like binoculars, and it has those little white circles in it. You hold it up to your face and click the orange tab, and it shows you pictures." ·

"A camera," I say.

"What?" Dean asks.

"It looks like a camera. Not binoculars."

"I always thought it was binoculars."

"You're supposed to be pretending to take pictures," I point out. "That's the whole clicking thing. You don't click binoculars."

"Alfredo Balli Trevino," Xavier suddenly says.

"What?" Dean and I ask, turning toward him.

Xavier looks away from the pig, a familiar look on his face. It's a somewhat distant expression, as if he didn't fully realize he was saying the words or didn't expect anyone to respond to them.

"You said Hannibal Lecter. He was fictional. A figment of the imagination. But he was based on a man named Alfredo Balli Trevino. The author, who created Hannibal Lecter, met him in a prison when he was researching another serial killer. He thought Trevina was a prison doctor because he had treated the serial killer's gunshot wound. It wasn't until later that he found out Trevino was a murderer. It was said that his skills as a surgeon let him fit his victims into very small boxes," Xavier says.

He meets my eyes for a brief second, then continues down the path.

"Happy Halloween," Dean says as he walks past Sam, who does not look amused by the story.

We make our way further and go around a curve deeper into the woods. It feeds out into what looks like a room without a ceiling. The walls on either side are splattered with fake blood and cracked with hatchet marks. Dripping letters write out the old nursery rhyme about Lizzie Borden.

"Ah, good old Elizabeth," Sam says. He glances at me with a playful look. "We're friends, so I can call her that."

"Not good friends," Xavier says.

"Because she's dead?" he asks with a note of sarcasm.

"Because her name wasn't Elizabeth. They called her Lizzie because her name was Lizzie. Lizzie Andrew, named after her father."

"Oh," Sam says.

Xavier takes a step closer to the wall and examines the bloody words. "Poem's all wrong, too. First, Abby was not her mother. She was her step-mother. And whoever was wielding the hatchet—not an ax, a hatchet—didn't hit her forty times. Only nineteen. To the front of the head and the rest to the back after she fell. Andrew actually received fewer than that. Probably eleven blows. They crushed his head, split his face in half, and left his eyeball sitting on his cheek."

He turns around sharply to look at the other wall. His head tilts to the side, and he gets a confused expression on his face.

"What is it?" I ask.

"The second verse," he says. "I would think it would be on the other way." He shrugs. "But I suppose that wouldn't make it any better. Still would be inaccurate. 'Andrew Borden now is dead. Lizzie hit him on the head. Now in Heaven, he will swing. And on the gallows, she will swing.'"

He's still humming as he walks away down the path. Sam's head snaps over to me.

"How does he know that? Why does he know that?" he asks.

"We might have found Xavier's hobby," I say.

The trail takes up almost another half-an-hour of turns and morbid scenery. At nearly every stop, Xavier has a complaint about the accuracy of the depiction. I know it's starting to get to Sam, but I'm just relieved to not be the only one to have immediately noted the strange details and implausible choices.

Ahead of us, the woods stop, and the trail seems to lead out onto an old paved road. We're starting to follow it when Dean glances back over his shoulder.

"What's that?" he asks.

I see what he's pointing out, and I smile.

"Let's find out."

145

CHAPTER TWENTY-SIX

"I didn't know anything like this was back here," I say. "I thought this was just old fairgrounds."

The weathered sign on the side of the road directs us to Ashbury Hill Amusement Park. The cracked paved road moves away from the pumpkin patch and deeper into the woods. Rather than the hill going up, it goes down, leading us along a slight slope that opens out to the crumbling entrance.

"It's been here forever," Xavier says. "My family came to this park all the time when I was a little boy. We only lived a couple of hours from here. When I moved back to Harlan, I couldn't wait to come back."

"Because you love amusement parks," I say softly.

He nods, moving ahead of us as if he's walking through time. He approaches the gate comfortably, the familiarity obvious in every movement. It's as if he's holding his ticket and expecting someone to appear and take it from his hand so he can go inside.

"When did it close?" Sam asks.

Xavier shakes his head. "I don't know."

There's a chain across the entrance, but it's been cut, and Xavier walks straight through it. We follow him, letting him guide us out onto what was once a smooth road leading into the park. Buildings on either side have broken windows and grass growing up through the sidewalks in front. Looming at the end of the road is a Ferris wheel with all of the gondolas removed.

"Are you all right?" I ask.

Xavier looks at me. "Of course. Being here gives me peace."

I nod gently. "Okay."

"Hey!" A shout makes us whip around to see an angry-faced security officer stalking toward us down the road. "What do you think you're doing in here?"

"I'm sorry," I call over. "We were just walking and saw the sign. We were curious."

"Agent Griffin?" he asks, the light of recognition hitting his face.

"Officer Murray," I say when he gets close. He's with the Harlan Police Department and has been helping us in the cornfields. Friendly guy. Always has some sort of joke to share. "I didn't realize it was you."

"I didn't realize it was you, either. Who else do you have with you?"

"Sam and Dean and Xavier," I tell him.

"What are y'all doing out here?"

"We were just exploring at the pumpkin patch and found the haunted trail that brought us out here. Kind of got away from us a little bit. What are you doing out here?"

"When I'm off duty at the department, I do security for the pumpkin patch and corn maze. My boys loved the pumpkin patch growing up, so I kinda like revisitin' it every year. Keep it safe for the kids. Stop wayward miscreants from wandering off and going into closed areas," he says with a laugh.

I hang my head for a second. "Sorry. As I said, we were just up at the pumpkin patch and found the Haunted Trail, so we decided to walk down it."

"That's a hayride," he says. "They do it at night with lights and fog machines. Scare-actors."

"I think we got our fill of it during the day," I tell him. "But this place is pretty amazing. I never even realized it was here. All I've ever heard is that this was the fairgrounds."

"It's been closed a long time," the officer says. "Technically, it's still functional. Power and water would be on if they were hooked up. The rides are a bit beaten up now, but they were runnin' when they closed up shop. It just didn't get enough attention all the way out here. Now the town doesn't like to advertise having an abandoned amusement park. Not fittin' the image, and not worth the money to fix it up."

"Maybe lure miscreants?" Dean asks.

Officer Murray laughs. "Exactly. So, everybody pretty much acts like it doesn't exist. Every so often, there's talk of bringin' it back, but nothin' ever comes of it. A Halloween haunt a couple of years, but that's it. It just kinda sits here. It's hard to believe how alive it used to be. Now it's just a little creepy, isn't it?"

"I think it's beautiful," Xavier says, still gazing around as if he can see the park as it was when he was a child.

"Well, that fits with the season, I guess. I'm sorry, I wish I could let you folks wander around a bit, but you're not allowed in here. You're not even supposed to be on that trail. Let's get you back to the pumpkin patch," he says.

"I'm sorry if I caused you any trouble," I say.

"No trouble," he shrugs. "It's good to see you doing something other than sit in that conference room buried neck-deep in evidence."

"That's what I've been telling her," Sam says, wrapping his arm around my waist and cuddling me close. "A little break every now and then is good for her."

"We'll see," I say.

We make our way along an access road Officer Murray shows us. It brings us out right in front of the checkout stand for the pumpkin patch. Our pumpkins are piled up on one of the wooden counters lined up in front of the gate.

"I was wondering where you got off to," the hayride driver calls over. "I have your pumpkins right here."

"Thank you," I say.

Since I doubt the hotel will let me start filling up their hallway with pumpkins, we bring our haul to Xavier's house. I can absolutely see why Dean described it the way he did. It's pristinely decorated, but everywhere I look, there seems to be a knob or lever attached to one of Xavier's creations. I want to touch all of them.

But I stop myself. I have to remember I'm a guest in this ridiculousness, and it's been sitting dormant for a decade now, so the mechanics might not be as reliable as they once were. That brings my mind back to the theme park. Xavier talked about it as if he'd gone when he was an adult, but it looked as if no one had been there in far too many years before that.

We spend the rest of the afternoon carving some of the pumpkins and roasting their seeds. On the way to his house, I'd stopped at the grocery store to pick up a container of pumpkin pie spice, and I sprinkle the cut off lids of the jack-o'-lanterns.

"Why are you doing that?" Xavier asks.

"So, when you light a candle in it, it will smell like pumpkin pie," I say.

He reaches into the bag he brought home from the store and pulls out battery-operated tea lights. I can't help but laugh. I tip back into Sam's arms and let him hold me, surrounding me in flannel and warmth. I could just stay like this. I would never have to think about anything else and be happy.

The levity doesn't last for long. I knew it couldn't. Not with the world ticking by around me.

The next day, heaviness settles into my heart, dragging it down deep into me as I listen to my father tell me everything he can about The Order of Prometheus. He shouldn't be doing this. These are secrets he's supposed to keep, traditions and rituals kept sacred for so many years.

But this is an emergency. He knows that as well as I do. So he lifts the veil. It's not everything. He can't get into all of the details or explain everything to me because his chapter is different from the one in Harlan. But the more he tells me, the heavier I feel.

I'm discovering something about my father I never knew, but I don't want to know it. It feels uncomfortable and raw, like something I shouldn't see. A part of him that was supposed to be kept back, but now he is laying bare, and in doing so, exposing so many others.

I appreciate his willingness. I can only hope it helps.

After meeting with my father, I stop by the doughnut shop and then follow my familiar path to Millie's hospital room. She smiles when she sees the box.

"At least this time you're bringing me some real food," she says.

"I figure if I'm taking advantage of the fact that they are holding you hostage and you can't get away from me, I might as well compensate with a treat. And after having experienced a diet of hospital cuisine for a couple of days, I now commiserate with you completely and feel you deserve these more than ever," I smile.

"Did you bring jelly-filled?" she asks.

"Of course! What kind of a person do you think I am?"

She lifts one eyebrow at me. "Do you really want me to answer that?"

"Fair enough. And on that note," I say, reaching into the box and pulling out one of the powdered sugar-covered lemon-filled donuts, "I'll just dive right in."

"Let me guess; you're here to ask me about Sterling again. I still don't know where he is or what he's doing."

"That's actually not what I want to ask you about," I tell her honestly. "Nobody's been able to figure out where he is, so I'm letting you off the hook on that one."

"Good," she says. "I can't help you with what my brother is doing."

"How about your other brother?" I ask.

"Ron?" she asks.

"Yes," I say. I take a bite of my doughnut to give me a few seconds to come up with the right sequence of words. It doesn't come, so I just go with what tumbles out of my mouth first. "Before everything happened, Dean and I followed you away from the bank and saw you meeting up with Ron out by the cornfield."

She closes her eyes briefly, shaking her head as if she can't believe what she just heard. "That was you?"

"Yes," I say.

"I knew I heard somebody," Millie says.

"What were you doing out there?" I ask.

"I was just talking to Ron," she says.

"I know," I say. "But why? Why were you meeting out there?"

"He's my brother, Emma. We don't live terribly close together, so sometimes we meet up in between just to catch up."

"That didn't look as if you were just catching up. He looked angry," I say.

"They're my brothers. The bonds of brotherhood are tight," she says.

I nod and finish my doughnut. After a few more minutes of visiting, I leave. Dean, Xavier, and Sam meet up with me outside.

"Anything?" Dean asks.

"She said she just met with Ron out there because they don't live close to each other, so sometimes that's where they get together. When I questioned her about it, she said the bonds of brotherhood are tight."

"Why do you have that look as if what she said is significant?" Dean asks.

"Because she's their sister, not their brother. It's not brotherhood for her. And isn't that almost exactly what my father said about The Order? When I was in the hospital, and he was telling me he and the two generations before him were all members?"

"She was trying to tell you something," Xavier says.

"But we already know Sterling is in The Order and that Ron heads up FireStarter. What else could she be trying to say?" Sam asks.

"I don't know." I look at each of them. "What are you doing now?"

"Noah expects me at the precinct soon," Sam says. "I'm going over a few things with him to see if I can give him new insights."

"Xavier and I are open," Dean says.

"Good. I need you to research the temple. We still have no idea what's going on with it, and now that they've reduced the surveillance, it's getting urgent. We need to know the history of that building. The Order chose it for a reason. My father said the chapters like to choose buildings for their meeting that have historical significance and speak to the heart of the given chapter. Whatever that means. We need to find the heart of that building."

"I thought we were looking for the heart of the chapter," Dean says.

I look at Xavier.

"Let the snack choose you," he says.

"Absolutely."

CHAPTER TWENTY-SEVEN

It takes two hours to get to Rachel Duprey's office and another hour of cooling my heels in the waiting room, but finally, she strides out toward me. Her walk is exactly as you'd imagine from her contact page photo. Formal and precise. Trained and heavily controlled.

She flashes me a smile that fits right in with her posture and movement, extending her hand to shake mine when she is still several steps away. That's a manipulation tactic, whether she knows it or not, though I'm pretty confident she does. It shows focus, direct concentration on me rather than onanything else around her.

I play into it, walking toward her and meeting her with our hands clasped.

"Rachel Duprey," she introduces herself. "I hear you've been waiting to speak with me."

"Yes," I say. "Actually, we've already spoken. Agent Emma Griffin."

The smile disappears from Rachel's face. Her shoulders square off against me, and her jaw tightens as she lifts her chin in a show of strength and resilience. She's preparing herself for the same types of onslaughts she dealt with for years and managed to deflect from her father and her family.

"I believe I told you I had nothing more to say to you," she says.

"No, actually, you didn't say that," I counter.

"Then allow me to say it now. I am not discussing this with you. It's over, and I want it to remain that way. I hope you understand that. Good day, Agent Griffin."

She turns on her heel and starts back to her office. She's not getting away that easily. I follow after her.

"But I don't understand," I say.

At that, she stops. Her back stays to me for a moment. We're locked in a stalemate. Finally, she lets out a breath.

"Come with me," she says.

I follow her into her office, and she shuts the door behind me.

"I made myself extremely clear when you called me," she says. "Coming to my place of business is completely out of line."

"Is it?" I ask. "I thought your whole thing was helping people. I need help."

"You need help dragging my father through the mud? Dredging up something none of us wants to think about anymore? That nobody needs to have to deal with? It's over. Why do you have to bring it up again?" she asks.

"Because it's not over. There are still a lot of questions. And as I said, I'm investigating another case that might have to do with your father's past. I need to know everything I can," I tell her.

"This is ridiculous," she scoffs. "There's nothing for me to tell you because there is nothing for you to know. My father did nothing wrong. Never. It was just a gold-digging woman who saw the potential for a big payday, and it didn't work out for her. He had nothing to do with her."

"Then why did everybody say he did?" I ask.

"Not everybody," she says. "A few tasteless media outlets. People hungry for a salacious story. Political opponents wanting to get him out of the way. People who mattered never believed it. I never believed he had anything to do with her walking away."

"Because that's what you believe she did," I say.

"It's what she did," Rachel insists. "So, there's no reason to believe anything else. She left and started another life because she was too humiliated to face the community she attempted to deceive. The only thing anybody was ever able to say is that my father went to the same hotel where she was last seen. That was a very popular hotel at the time. A lot of people stayed there. He had a standing reservation. He was on a completely different floor from the one where she was staying. Nobody saw them together. Nobody saw them arrive together or leave together. Nobody can even prove he was there that night. Just that he always had a reservation."

"And can you prove he was somewhere else?" I ask.

"Yes," she nods. "As I told countless media outlets twenty years ago when any of this mattered, he was at a fundraiser. I have pictures of him with some of the other donors. Ironically enough, they are some of my favorite pictures of him. The light inside hadn't completely died yet."

"But you helped him get that light back, didn't you, Rachel?"

"You say that as if there's something wrong with it," she says. "I worked hard for my father. From the time I was a little girl, I knew he was going to be one of the most important men in the world. When that woman tried to tear him down, I made sure he got the revival he deserved. He was vindicated, and everyone got to see what an incredible man he was."

"What about Lilith?" I ask.

She visibly retracts in response to the name.

"What about her?" she asks.

"What was your relationship with your stepmother?"

"I don't even like to refer to her that way. She was a useless person who was never good for my father. Nothing ever satisfied her. She never had enough. Enough money. And things. Enough attention. It was just never enough. Then when Lindsey Granger came along, Lilith jumped on the opportunity to play the withering scorned wife in front of my father and lapped up the attention for being strong and standing by him in public."

"So, she believed it," I note.

"Yes. You know, there was a time when I thought she might be responsible for Lindsey's disappearance. Before I realized what actually happened. There were a few newspapers that ran editorials wondering if dear Lilith might have offed her." Rachel crosses her arms over her chest and cocks her hip to the side. "I almost wish she had. Then I wouldn't ever have to deal with either of them again."

"Do you know where Lilith is?"

"No," she answers quickly. "And I don't care. The instant my father died, she was no longer related to me."

"What happened to the inheritance?" I ask.

"What business is that of yours?" she asks. "Not that any of this is."

"It's just a question. It's public knowledge your father left you the bulk of his estate."

"Yes," Rachel nods. "Because he knew the type of woman Lilith actually was."

"But that still left a considerable amount of money for her."

"More than she deserved," she confirms.

I nod. "How did your father die, Rachel?"

Her face goes dark, and her arms slide down her body to hang in fists at her sides.

"Get out. How dare you come into my office and try to pry into the most painful moment of my life? Get out of my office, and don't let me catch you digging into my private matters anymore. Leave me and my father's memory alone. Don't call again. Either of you."

"Have a good evening, Rachel," I say.

I start toward the door, unswayed by her threats.

My phone is in my hand before I get to the car. Rachel said not to call again. Either of us.

I don't even have to ask what that means. I call Lydia. There's no answer. That's odd, so I hang up and call again. And again, it rings several times before going to voicemail. That's very strange. Every time I've seen Lydia, she has been obsessive about her phone. She checks it every few seconds, gripping it hard at her side or in her lap if she isn't on it.

I've never seen her phone ring and have her ignore it. This is especially true if she thinks that she's on the path of something.

Of course, it's entirely possible she's just ignoring me. She might know I would eventually find out that she called Rachel and doesn't want to hear me tell her to back off anymore. At least, not until she has something she thinks will compel me to bring her into the investigation.

I don't have the time or the patience to worry too much about what Lydia is doing. Instead, I call the guys.

"It'll be a couple of hours before I get back to the hotel," I tell Dean. "Sam has his phone off, so if you talk to him, will you let him know?"

"Don't go to the hotel. Meet us at Xavier's house," Dean tells me. "We called the precinct and left a message for Sam, so he'll know when he gets done with the detective."

"What's going on?" I ask.

"We might have found something interesting."

CHAPTER TWENTY-EIGHT

SIX MONTHS AFTER DEATH...

She would be unrecognizable now. If anyone even knew she was there and came to find her, no one would know it was her.

All that was left that might link her to what someone remembered was her decaying clothing and some wisps of hair. Perhaps the ring that once meant so much. He didn't know she was still wearing it. Maybe if he had, he would have taken it back. Maybe if he had, she wouldn't be here.

Her beauty was gone. From the time she was very young, she was told not to rely on her looks. One day they would be gone. But no one ever thought it would be like this.

The cold weather was gone now. Her grave had gone through two seasons. Chilly fall rain became ice around her. For a short time, it seemed it might hold tight to her. That it might keep her as she was. But that couldn't last forever. The spring came. It always would.

With the warmth came the thaw. And more people. More voices. Everywhere around her, there were more people, but nobody knew.

They walked right over her. Lay beside her. Laughed and shouted. Worked and bled.

But not one ever knew she was there. Not one stopped to notice her.

CHAPTER TWENTY-NINE

"So, we went to City Hall, and they weren't a lot of help", Dean explains. "Turns out, all the property records from the town dated from a certain year backward are all kept in deep storage. Essentially it would take weeks to be able to find a deed or any other documents having to do with the temple."

"Okay," I say. "So, did you ask for them to find it for you?"

"We did," he says. "But we didn't stop there. I couldn't imagine you would want to wait weeks for people to find this information for you, so we had an idea. We might not be able to find the ownership information right at this moment, but we can find out more about the building."

"How?" I ask.

"The library," Xavier cuts in. "That's where all the old memories of town are held. Where they put them, so people won't forget."

"There are reference books in the library for all the historical buildings throughout town. The old hotel. The original post office. Some of the old houses. All the information," Dean translates. "When they were built, who originally lived in them or used them. And blueprints."

"Blueprints?" I raise an eyebrow.

"Well, not necessarily blueprints," he acknowledges. "But plans. Drawings of the layout of the buildings. Some of them from the original plans. Of course, some of these buildings have been modified many times over since they were originally built, but it's the basic structure. The original concept of what each building was."

"Did you find the temple?" I ask.

Xavier nods. "We remembered everything."

I walk with the two of them into a large formal dining room where a massive table is spread with large photocopies. Standing over them, I see they are several sets of plans for the building. Alongside them are old maps of the city.

"What am I looking at?" I ask Dean.

"You probably already guessed it, but the temple was originally a church. Built more than two-hundred years ago as one of the first buildings in this area. Before the concept of the town of Harlan even existed. The church was much smaller then, but the sanctuary is actually original. So are a couple of the rooms. Essentially, the center of the building is the original church. Over the years, different groups expanded it. Then when The Order of Prometheus took over, they expanded even further. But there was one section they didn't modify."

"What section?" I ask.

Xavier points to one of the images. "The basement."

"Do you notice something odd about it?" Dean asks.

I'm staring at it, trying to figure out what he's pointing out to me when Sam comes into the room. He leans down and kisses my cheek.

"Hey, sweetie," I smile.

"What are we looking at?" he asks, poring over the map.

"I'm not sure," I tell him. "They think they might have found something about the temple. But I'm not catching on to it."

"Look," Dean says. "Look at the original pictures and then this one."

I look at the buildings, my eyes going back and forth. There's something but can't put my finger on it.

Sam suddenly leans down closer, turning one of the pictures so that he can look at it at a better angle.

"They're not in the same place," he notes. "Is that just something wrong with the drawing?"

"No," Xavier says. "They are, and they aren't. A basement in a basement. A door that isn't a door."

"This is the original basement," Dean says, outlining the area of the building with his finger on the original depiction of the church. "And this is the basement about a hundred and fifty years after the church was built. It's bigger and higher up in the building. not by much, but enough to keep the original one hidden."

"Why would they want to do that?" I ask.

"What year was the basement modified? Sam asks.

"Nineteen twenty," Dean says.

Realization dawns on me.

"Oh, holy shit. It's a speakeasy."

"That would be correct," Dean grins, his satisfaction at keeping me guessing clearly obvious on his face. "And if you will turn your attention to the maps of the city that my good buddy Xavier analyzed for me, you will notice some very strategic construction happening around the town at that time."

Xavier steps up and starts pointing out buildings and their arrangement throughout the town. Using his fingertip, he draws lines between the various buildings and the temple, then each of them and the river.

"Tunnels," Sam says. "There are rum-running tunnels."

"*Documented* rum-running tunnels," Dean adds, pulling out another piece of paper and showing me a scan from a book on the history of the area. "It doesn't mention the temple. Probably for obvious reasons. But it says that the bootlegging activity in this area was legendary. The proximity to the river and the woods made it easy to create and transport alcohol without anybody noticing. Now according to this, almost all of the buildings that contain those tunnels have been destroyed. The only tunnel that is recognized goes from the basement of the original hotel to a spot out by the river where there was a house. And that tunnel has been sealed."

"But what if there are other ones?" I say. "Ones they don't talk about."

"Exactly," Dean says.

"A door that isn't a door," Xavier says.

"A basement that isn't the basement," I say.

"A place to hide and a place you can go where no one will know what you've done," Sam says.

"I think the heart of the building showed itself to you," I say.

"So, when are we going?" Sam asks.

None of us can wait for the morning. It's dark and cold, but we dress in layers, get flashlights, and head to the temple. If the guys are right, this explains how the members were able to get out without being spotted. Then how they were able to get back in and out again, even when the building was under surveillance. It changes everything.

There are no officers on duty as we approach the building. Now that we've been inside, we know better how to navigate it. The only problem is the heavy padlock on the door.

"What do we do about this?" Sam asks.

"We had a search warrant," I tell him. "We were granted access."

"Does it cover now?" Sam asks.

"I don't have the paper in front of me," I admit.

"As long as we're on the same page," he says.

"Dean?" I say.

He gives a single nod. "Let's go."

He leads us around the side of the building and into the cellar he originally brought me into.

"Convenience," I comment. "Can't get enough of it."

"Alright," Dean says. "We have to figure out how to access the original basement. Remember, it's not going to be easy to find. These doors were hidden. Even people who frequented the building probably didn't know what was going on right downstairs."

"What happens if it's sealed?" I ask.

"What happens if it's not?" Xavier asks.

I reach over and let the back of my hand touch the back of his. He moves one finger around to squeeze mine. That's enough.

"Dean, you and Xavier go to one side. Sam and I are going to go to the other. Keep your flashlights on and your phones accessible. If you find anything, let us know. But be aware there might be people in this building that we don't know about," I tell them.

We part ways, and Sam holds my hand tightly as we walk through the dark basement, searching for any indication of a passageway. We sweep our phone lights slowly back and forth, up the walls and into the hallway, looking for something—anything. But all we see are cobwebs and dust.

A few times, I think I catch the flash of movement, but it's just a bug skittering away from the light. We scour every inch methodically, once, twice. But nothing. An hour in, I'm losing hope when I notice a piece of furniture up against the wall I hadn't seen.

"What is that?" I ask. I keep looking at it, trying to figure out why it's there.

"It's an old desk," Sam says. We walk toward it, and he shines his flashlight on it. "A really old desk."

I walk up to the side of it and run my fingers down along the edge.

"It's attached to the wall," I say. "Why would they attach a desk like this to the wall?"

Sam hands me his flashlight. "Hold this."

He runs his hand over the roll-top portion of the desk, then along the edge. He goes back and does it again, pausing when he reaches one corner.

"Did you find anything?" I ask.

"Maybe," he says. "I read a book once that told about a desk that had a hidden slot. If the pieces were arranged exactly right, it unlocked a latch. There's something loose here."

I move to shine more light where he's looking. I can see a piece of wood that looks slightly different from the others.

"Look," I point. "That dip of wood right there. It looks as if it's been worn down from being touched a lot."

"Get the guys," Sam says.

I set his flashlight down on the top of the desk and make my way back across the cellar. I'm using my phone as a flashlight, but if I can't find Dean and Xavier, so I call for them. Fortunately, I don't have to search far. They're only a few dozen yards away from us.

"Hey," I tell them. "Sam thinks he's found something. Come on."

We turn around, but by the time we get back to the desk, Sam isn't there.

"Where is he?" Xavier asks.

"I don't know," I say. "He was right here."

"Move the desk," Sam's voice comes from the dark.

It startles me, but I step up to the side of the desk and press on it. It shifts slightly, and both men come up behind me and take hold of the furniture, shifting it easily out of place.

It swings into the rest of the room, revealing a small gap in the stone. I shine my flashlight into it and see four steps leading down. Sam's face is at the bottom.

"Found it," he says.

Dean lets out a celebratory laugh, and we start down the steps, but I notice Xavier isn't following.

"Should we leave a note?" he asks. "Just in case we get lost down there?"

"The only people who would find a note we left are the ones who would just as soon seal us in," Dean points out.

Xavier nods and gives a half-shrug, knowing this makes complete sense, and steps forward without hesitation. I go down first, followed by Xavier. Dean stays at the top to swing the desk back into place. As soon as the door closes, inky, almost tangible blackness presses in around us. It absorbs the light from our phones and flashlights so we can see only inches around us.

Pitch black.

"Well, isn't this just scary as all get out," Dean mutters.

"Thank you for the slogan for our journey," I reply.

"Where do we go?" Sam asks.

"There's only one direction," I say, nodding straight ahead. "Let's find out who was helping the lost flock drown their sorrows in demon rum."

CHAPTER THIRTY

The tunnel is dark and dingy. The stone walls radiate the cold back to us, so I shiver despite the layers I packed on. As we move down the stairs, a creepy feeling crawls up and down my spine. It almost feels like there are other people in here with us, even though I can't see them.

Occasionally, one of us flashes one of our lights behind us and to either side. We all feel the same thing. As if eyes are skittering along the wall after us. The tunnel itself is alive. It knows we're there, and it's tracking our every movement.

We've been walking for almost half an hour when we get to a dip in the wall. Sam stops and places his hand on it.

"I think this used to be an offshoot of the tunnel," he says. "It's been bricked up; you can see the different patterns." He shows us with his light.

"Keep going," I announce. "The way in front of us is open, so we keep going. Until something stops us."

"I don't like the way you said 'something,'" Dean comments.

"Trick-or-treat," I murmur.

We keep going. Behind me, I can hear Xavier humming. There's no particular tune, just a sound that occasionally dips or swells. I don't know if he's giving himself a soundtrack or just trying to fill the space around us. Either way, I'm grateful for it. The silence is too deep. It's the type of silence that makes anxiety slink up inside you, and makes your muscles stiffen up with anticipation as you just wait for that sound that'll scare you.

I can only hope it's just a sound.

It isn't lost on me that this could be more than just a tunnel. Whatever purpose it originally served, it could have been modified just as the basement was modified. At any point, we could come out to an underground room or a trap. We might not be alone down here.

With every step, I get ready. I prepare myself for what might come next. There isn't much space here. There are points in the tunnel where we have to walk single file, and some places that force us to duck down to get through. If something does happen, it's going to be hard to get away.

"Xavier," I say. "Are you doing okay?"

"Would it make any difference if I wasn't?" he asks.

I laugh. "I guess not."

"We'll get there," he says. "We will get there."

A few minutes later, Sam stops in front of me. I crash into his back and clutch onto his shirt.

"What's wrong?" I ask.

"The tunnel ahead of us," he says. "It's partially collapsed."

I look around him and shine my light forward. It joins up with the beams from Dean and Sam, and I can see where part of the tunnel has come down. Rocks and rubble litter the floor and create a small space to move through.

"What do we do?" Dean asks. "Do we turn back?"

"I'm not," I tell them. "I can get through that."

"You might jostle something out of place," Dean says.

"I won't," I say.

"Emma," Sam whispers, but I look up at him.

"Let me do this, Sam. I've got it. Trust me."

I give him a kiss on the cheek, then walk around them toward the gap in the rocks.

"What if you do?" Xavier calls after me.

I look over my shoulder at him.

"Run like hell."

I walk carefully toward the rocks. With each step, I listen and watch to check for any movement. Nothing happens. I slowly approach the opening and rest my hand against the solid section of the wall. Crouching down, I lift one leg and slither my way through the entrance. I hold my breath and try to keep steady. No shaking. Just slow, deliberate motion. My back hits one of the rocks, loosening it and making it drop. As it slides away, I dive forward out to the other side just as it kicks up a cloud of dust with a loud thump.

"Are you alright?" Sam calls.

I stand up from where I landed on my knees and turn to check the entrance. It looks like only that one rock fell. I move to go back toward it, so I can help the guys through. I'm about to reach through the opening when another chunk comes down, sending more dust flying.

"Emma!"

The sound of Sam screaming my name is more chilling than the rocks collapsing down on each other. When the dust settles, the tunnel is almost completely blocked. I can still see some of a flashlight beam dancing through, but it's not enough to fit through.

"It's too dangerous to touch those rocks again," I call back. "They could shift, and we don't know what would happen."

"What are we supposed to do?" Dean asks. "We can't just leave you over there."

"Yes, you can," I say. "Turn around and go back up the tunnel. Go back into the temple. Xavier, did you bring the map?"

"Yes," he says.

"Show them where the tunnel goes. Figure it out. I'll meet you there," I tell them, fighting to keep my voice steady.

"What if the rest of the tunnel is sealed?" Dean asks.

"I'll meet you there," I repeat.

"Emma," Sam says.

"I love you," I say.

173

Turning my back to the collapsed rocks, I shine my flashlight ahead of me and start to walk. Behind me, I don't hear anything. The men haven't moved from where they were standing.

"Go!" I shout back. "Get out of here!"

I finally hear their footsteps retreating, and mine mimic theirs as they get further and further apart. Soon, I hear nothing but my own breath.

The tunnel continues to get narrower as I make my way down it. Soon I can open my arms only a few inches to the side and run the backs of my hands across the rough stone. My face aches with the cold, and my lungs feel as if they are filling with dust and dirt. I focus on my breaths, thinking about them rather than anything else.

The silence is horrifying, but I tell myself it's better than hearing something. If I hear something, that means I'm not alone. That's not what I want. I want to hear nothing. I want the silence.

Until I hear it. Ahead of me. I can't tell what it is. But it's something. There's a sound in the distance. I have no choice but to move toward it. It's either that or stay exactly where I am. and I'm not the type to stand still.

One hand still wrapped around my phone, I put the other close to my gun and continue down the tunnel. The sound gets louder. High-pitched and thin. Almost like wailing. It takes me a few minutes to realize what it is. Wind.

There's air moving across an opening somewhere. My footsteps get faster. I run toward the sound. Finally, the light of my phone hits what looks like a broken wooden step. The risers above it are broken as well, but the one on top seems solid. I step up on it and feel around for a handle or knob that'll open the hatch.

I find it, but it's too heavy to move with one hand. I reluctantly push my phone down into the neckline of my sweatshirt, pushing it into place inside my tank top, so I don't drop it. The darkness surrounds me, almost suffocating. My heart beats faster. I can feel the wind now. There's a gap on one side of the hatch, just enough to let the air move over it and create the wailing sound.

As my eyes adjust, I realize that it is also letting in just a hint of light. It's not much, but it's enough to give me hope. I shove against the hatch with every bit of my weight and strength. Finally, it gives way. I force it aside and scramble up.

Pulling my phone back out of my shirt, I shine a light around me. I'm in another basement, but not like the one I was in before. It's empty except for a few broken pieces of furniture stuffed up against the walls. There's a quiet feeling here. Desolate. Abandoned.

Ahead of me, there is a set of stairs leading up, but to the side, light shines down through the broken half of a set of storm doors. I run for them and climb out into the night air. I look around, drawing in the fresh breaths as fast as I can without making myself pass out. I'm in what looks like an overgrown yard and behind me is a run-down house.

A few yards away from the house, I drop down into the grass. My phone rings in my hand, and I almost sob with relief.

"The one time I can get reception," I answer.

"Are you okay?" Sam asks.

"I'm okay. I'm out. Are you on your way?"

Headlights sweep across my face, and I stand up. For an instant, my heart freezes.

"I see you," Sam says.

I let out the breath I was holding and start toward the car. It's barely stopped when the passenger door opens, and he throws himself out, running toward me. His arms clamp tight around me, one hand clutching my hair.

"I told you I'd meet you here," I whisper.

"Wherever you are, I will be there," he whispers back. "Always."

"Emma, I am so glad to see you," Dean calls over as he exits the driver's side.

"You, too," I tell him.

"Did you notice where we are?" Sam asks.

I shake my head. "Where are we?"

"See those trees?" he asks, pointing into the distance and a dark row of trees against the deep blue horizon.

"Yeah," I say.

"Right on the other side is Lilith's house."

I look back at him with widened eyes. "That can't be a coincidence."

"You know what I always say," he murmurs.

We say it in unison:

"There are no coincidences."

CHAPTER THIRTY-ONE

The next morning, I still feel as if the cold from the tunnel hasn't completely left me. I'm wrapped up in a blanket, sitting on my hotel room bed, going over my notes and piecing things together, when Sam comes in.

"I told Detective White everything," he says. "You're going to have to talk to Creagan, but we're going to figure out a way to make the discovery of that tunnel admissible."

"It has to be," I say. "That's how they got out. It's how they took everything from the building. That's tampering with evidence."

"If we can prove that there was a crime," Sam points out.

I let out a sigh and nod. "There's always that."

"We just have to link them to verifiable criminal activity," he muses. "We just have to find where they slipped up."

Dean pokes his head into the room.

"Am I interrupting?" he asks.

"No, come in," I say. "Did you get them?"

"Right here," he offers.

"What is that?" Sam asks as I take the folder from Dean.

"Hopefully, the resolution to my curiosity," I say.

"I'm going to need more information than that," Sam says.

The door opens again, and Xavier comes in. His arms are full of different cans of drinks from the vending machine down the hallway. Each of his pockets contains a different kind of snack.

"You settling in for the long haul?" Sam asks.

"Just couldn't decide," Xavier tells him.

"And sometimes you don't have to," I say.

He empties all the goodies out onto the other bed and sits down to start arranging them. I watch him for a few seconds, trying to figure out his organizational technique, but I can't. I turn my attention back to the folder and look at Sam.

"I just can't stop thinking about the Prometheus members' reaction when Dean said I was already claimed by Dragon. He said it with complete confidence, and they totally believed him. There wasn't a single person in that room who wasn't completely convinced I was not already promised in some way to the Dragon," I say.

"So, he's a good liar," Sam says. "I think that is part of the job description of a private investigator, isn't it?"

Dean shoots him a glare. Some other time, I will wax poetic about how nice it is to see two of the most important men in my life finally starting to get along. But right now, I have to keep this train of thought moving forward.

"It's not that they believed his lie because he was confident," I continue. "He didn't walk in there and say I was owed to Peter Christopherson just hoping that one of them would think that name sounded compelling enough. He used the word Dragon. And every single person in that room reacted. They were afraid. Compelled to show respect. There wasn't a single question or moment of hesitation. They know who he is."

"But he's been dead for years," Sam counters. "Is it possible they knew who he was before? That he had something to do with The Order before you investigated him?"

"No," I say. "I mean, he might have been connected to The Order, but that's not what they were reacting to. This was not the reaction of a group of people who either knew a person was dead or who hadn't heard from them in years. And that got me thinking."

"About what?"

"His death," I say.

"It's easy to fool someone when you're the only one watching," Xavier says.

"Something like that," I say. I open the folder and flip through the information. "Remember I told you he died in a crash of a prison transport van? He was the only prisoner being transported at the time. The body inside was so horrifically burned and mangled, there were no features available to be compared visually, but the driver walked away with only a slight burn and a broken wrist."

"How is that possible?" Sam asks.

"I don't know, but does that sound familiar to you at all?" I ask.

"It sounds like Mason Goldman," he says.

"Exactly. A body burned beyond recognition. Identified based on circumstantial evidence." I flip through the pages and pull out the one I am looking for. Slapping it flat down on the comforter, I point out the bottom line.

"Both death acknowledgements were signed by Judge Sterling Jennings. He's alive. All this time, he's been alive."

"What does it mean?" Dean asks. "What would the Dragon have to do with The Order?"

"How many times do you think I can visit somebody in the hospital before the administration blacklists me?" I ask.

As it turns out, I don't even get the opportunity to risk being banned from any future visitation. When I step out of the elevator, Gloria gives me her usual bright smile.

"How's your arm feeling?" she asks.

"Good," I say, lying through my teeth.

The truth is my arm hurts, and I've just had to get used to it. When all this is over, I'll rest it. Until then, I need both arms.

"Great to hear," she smiles. "And in another bit of good news, Millie was discharged."

I was on my way around the nurse's station to her room, but I stop.

"Discharged? When?" I ask.

"Early this morning. She's doing so much better," she says.

I manage a smile. "Good. That's good. I'm really glad to hear that."

I'm worried as I ride the elevator back down and walk to my car. Something tickles the back of my brain. I reach for my phone to call her, but before I can, it rings. It's not Millie. The name that shows up is far more of a shock and that.

"Hello?"

"When I told you to leave me alone, I meant all your little friends, too," Rachel Duprey growls through the phone.

"What are you talking about?" I ask.

"Please don't act stupid," she says. "I already have to encounter enough idiots in my daily life. I don't need somebody else behaving like one. You know exactly what I'm talking about."

"Actually, I don't. I've had a few things on my mind other than you."

"Don't talk about my family," she seethes. "Don't contact me or try to research my father or me. Don't even *think* our names. What you are doing is reprehensible. I've looked into you, Emma Griffin. I know about your past. Think about how it would make you feel if somebody kept dragging up your mother's death over and over again."

"Ms. Duprey, I have no idea what you are talking about. I've been busy investigating my case."

"If I hear from you or that woman Lydia again, I will be in contact with my lawyer. I'm tired of being harassed with all these questions," she says.

"Ms. Duprey, I didn't—"

The call ends abruptly, and I sit in my car for a few seconds, just going over the conversation in my mind. Shaking my head, I dial Lydia. At this point, she hasn't just aggravated me and possibly compromised the investigation. She's conjured up a potential lawsuit. It's probably not something I can stop, but the least I can do is warn her about it.

But she won't answer her phone. Still.

I grab my computer from where I keep it tucked under the front seat and open it up. Lydia's cold case database website is bookmarked, making it easy to pull it up quickly. I don't see anything new on it, but when I go to the contact page, I'm able to connect with several of the other contributors.

They each respond to my messages within seconds. Not one of them has heard from Lydia within the last couple of days. None knows where she is.

It's concerning, and I'm really starting to worry until a thought flashes into my mind. I know exactly where she is.

Setting my phone in its stand on my dashboard, I connect to Bluetooth and call Sam.

"Babe, I just wanted to let you know I will probably be gone for most of the afternoon," I say.

"What are you doing?" he asks.

"Apparently, Lydia Walsh has been calling Rachel Duprey and asking her a bunch of questions. Now Rachel is threatening to sue us. Lydia won't answer her phone, and none of her friends at the database knows where she is. Which tells me there's only one place she is. If I'm right, I need to get to her before she causes us any more trouble. It's about an hour away, but I'll keep in touch with you. Is everything doing okay on your end?"

"Everything's fine," he says. "The forensic team was able to reconstruct three of the skeletons from the cornfield. There are a couple of small pieces missing, but it's enough to return to the families."

"Good," I tell him. "Let me know when we know their names."

"I love you," he says.

"I love you too."

CHAPTER THIRTY-TWO

TWO WEEKS DEAD ...

She wasn't protected where she lay. The insects still found her.
The sheet around her was nothing but a veil.
But it was the only one she would ever wear.
The ground became her altar.
She had already begun to transform, to offer herself up.
Pale to green to red to black.
Soon only white.
There were still questions above ground. People were still asking where she was.
Maybe he hoped she would be found.
Maybe he hoped she wouldn't.
Two weeks dead, straddling reality. Her name still in people's mouths. Her face still in their minds. But her body becoming one with the earth.

CHAPTER THIRTY-THREE

A little more than an hour later, I pull into the parking lot of the Garden View Hotel. I can immediately see what Rachel meant when she said it used to be a popular hotel. The shell of something grand and beautiful is still there, but it's been battered with time and neglect.

It isn't completely derelict, but it's obviously not what it used to be. I park in one of the many available spots and walk under a sagging portico into the lobby. There's a cavernous feel to it. There should be more people to take up the space.

Not just the physical space. But the energy of it. The air. There should be more sound, more vibration of existence.

Instead, it's just still.

I cross the lobby to the front desk. A woman standing behind it looks up at me and offers a hopeful smile.

"Good afternoon," she says. "Welcome to the Garden View. My name is Cheryl. How long will you be staying with us?"

"Actually, I'm not getting a room. Can I speak with the manager?"

She looks at me with a flicker of hurt in her eyes, and I smile at her in what I hope is a reassuring way.

"Sure," she says. "I'll be right back."

She walks into an office behind the desk, and a few seconds later, a man comes out. He walks up to the desk with a smile that feels just a little off.

"Hello," he says. "My name is David Robinson; I'm the manager of this hotel. How can I help you?"

"Hi," I say. "I'm actually looking for somebody who I think is staying here. I haven't been able to get in touch with her, and I need to speak with her."

"And what is your name?" he asks.

"Emma Griffin," I say.

His eyes lift to me with an incredulous expression.

"Agent Emma Griffin?" he asks.

"Yes," I say, my eyebrows sliding toward each other as I narrow my eyes at him. "How did you know that?"

"I was actually getting ready to call you," he says.

"Why?" I ask.

This visit is already not off to the most reassuring of starts.

"We have a guest who we had not heard from in almost two days. We entered her room and found it empty," he says. "But her personal items were still here.

"Lydia," I say, letting out a breath with her name.

"Yes," he says. "While we were looking for her, phone calls came from you to her phone. I was going to ask you to come here and claim her belongings."

Part of me feels that is just a subtle way for him to say he wants me to settle-up her bill. What I'm more worried about is where Lydia is and why she hasn't been seen or heard from.

"Is everything still in her room?" I ask.

"Yes," he says. "We left it just as it was except for checking her phone."

"Can I go up and see it?"

"Yes, of course. But you understand, I will need to accompany you," he says.

This feels like the beginning of a movie I don't want to be a part of, but I agree anyway. It's the only way I'm going to be able to get into her room and figure out what happened to her. Robinson steps back into the office for a second and comes back with a key card. I follow him to the elevator, and we go up to the third floor.

"It's just right here," he says, guiding me to the fourth room down the hall. He uses the key card to access the room. I step inside, and the room feels as if Lydia was just there. There's a lingering perfume smell in the air, and her suitcase is open on one of the beds.

"No housekeeping came in?" I ask.

"They did but noticed she hadn't even used the beds."

I sift through her suitcase and the drawers. Her computer is here, along with the small notebook she carries with her. On its own, that is disturbing.

"And she didn't say anything unusual to anyone?" I ask.

"No," he says. "She checked in and did not interact with the staff again. We do have our suspicions that she left the hotel, perhaps to avoid her bill."

"Why would you think that?" I ask.

"Surveillance footage shows her movements," he says.

"You have surveillance footage? Can I see it?"

"Come with me," Robinson says.

I leave all of Lydia's belongings in her room and follow the manager down to the security office.

The manager presses *play* on the footage and zooms in the first camera that catches Lydia. She comes into frame from the bottom, moving up the hall rather normally at first. Then she stumbles for a moment and stops to regain her composure. One hand goes to the wall, and she continues her steps, her fingertips tracing the way as she walks.

"This is the first time she shows up on the footage. She must have come in from one of the outside doors directly into this hall," the manager explains.

"Are there a lot of those?" I ask.

"Only in that part of the hotel. The others are locked for safety purposes. They have loud alarm systems on them now, so no one uses them unless it's an emergency."

I nod and continue watching. Pointing at the screen, I look over at the manager again.

"It says 'stairs' here, with an arrow. Is that stairwell accessible?" I ask.

"Sure, but hardly anyone ever uses it, aside from exercise nuts who want to get steps in and people looking for a semi-private place to get kinky," he says. I don't like the way his lip curls up in a grin at the end of that sentence. The grossness of his grin radiates off him like too much cologne.

"Are there cameras in the stairwells?"

"No," he says after a moment's hesitation. I decide to let that one slide for now.

Lydia continues down the hall until she is out of view of the camera, and Mr. Robinson clicks the mouse. The view changes to another camera. This time Lydia is coming down from the top of the frame. As she gets about halfway down the hall, she suddenly stops and spins around. She is facing away from the camera, but it seems as if her jaw is moving as she's talking to someone.

"Is anyone else in the hall with her?" I ask.

"No, the other camera, if you look on that screen, shows the first camera. It's empty. It looks like she's talking to herself, right?"

I don't respond but sit back in my chair to keep watching. As Lydia makes her way down the halls, she begins to act more and more erratically. She begins to zigzag in the hall, occasionally bouncing off the wall and stumbling a bit. Once or twice she looks as if she's half-heartedly trying a couple of doors, but they don't open, so she continues.

The next camera I see shows a wide shot of a hallway with a dead end. Elevators line the wall the camera is facing, and Lydia comes from the bottom of the screen. She trips and falls down but gets herself back up quickly, ducking behind a large plant and hiding like a child. Only there is no playfulness there.

"She must have been wasted," David comments, but I ignore him.

Lydia peeks her head out from behind the plant and looks back down the hall in the direction she came from. Then, sneaking out, she crosses over to the other wall and ducks behind it. She looks back down the hall again before turning away toward one of the ends of the hallway where the camera doesn't see. It looks as if she is still talking.

"Where is this part of the hotel?" I ask.

"Deep in the East Wing. That's what's so odd. We rarely have anyone staying down there."

Lydia continues her conversation with whatever she thinks she's seeing, then looks back down the hall again. She seems to relax, as if whatever is chasing her stopped. Then something gets her attention from behind her, off beside the elevators where she had been speaking before, and she wanders that way, disappearing from view.

"And that's it," David says.

"What do you mean, 'that's it'? Where is the next camera?" I ask.

"There are none. That end of the hotel is blocked off to guests. Boarded up, even. Those elevator doors don't even open. It's why we don't put people in those rooms often; that part of the hotel isn't really used."

"So, she just disappears?" I ask, my voice rising in frustration.

"Essentially, yes," he nods, but there is something in his eyes. Something I can't quite read.

"Essentially," I repeat. "Have you searched the hotel?"

"Of course we have," he says, sounding slightly offended.

"Have you? Personally?" I ask. There is a moment where he stares at me and blinks. Then he nods.

"Yes, but if you would like, I can take you out there, and you can see for yourself. She vanished without a trace at that point."

"Let's go," I say, standing. Something isn't adding up. People don't just vanish.

Mr. Robinson leads me down to the hallway from the video, and we begin to walk slowly down it. As we reach the area I recognize from the first clip, I see a door leading to the outside. There is an emergency bar on it, but it looks as if it's compressed permanently.

"Is this the door you were talking about?" I ask. "Where she got in?"

"Yes, it is used fairly often, so we disabled the emergency lock," he says dismissively. As if all hotels have doors that are randomly left unlocked.

We keep walking, and I touch the walls where I remember her fingers tracing. I look back over my shoulder at times when I remember her doing the same. But nothing stands out. It's just a hotel hallway.

"This is where she fell against the wall," the manager points, a note of disdain in his voice. "Whatever she was on was affecting her balance pretty badly."

I peer ahead to the end of the hallway. The bank of useless elevators sits, gold paint peeling away from what I am sure were once impressive columns. I make my way directly to the area where Lydia was seen last. When we get there, I turn to where she went. There is a blank wall, a utility closet, the door missing, and nothing else other than disheveled equipment leaned against the wall in various places.

"What's all this?" I ask, pointing at the buckets and boxes lying around.

"Ah, just remnants from when the remodel was in full effect. Since no one stays on this side of the hotel, there was no rush to clean up when they abandoned it."

"Were they working on the elevators?" I ask.

"Among other things," he says. There is a caginess in his response.

Something catches my eye, and I step closer to it. Behind one of the large pieces of plywood leaning against the wall is another door. It is newer and cheap, but the lock looks solid.

"Where does this door go?" I ask.

"Oh, that? That's locked. It has been locked for ages."

"Where does it go, Mr. Robinson?" I ask again, this time, my voice dropping a little.

"I told you, it is locked."

I turn toward him, and my expression must say all the words that are needed.

"But, if you like, I am sure I have a key."

CHAPTER THIRTY-FOUR

As Mr. Robinson searches for the key, I move the plywood out of the way, shoving some buckets as well.

"You see all the stuff that's here. It's been in that exact spot for months, at least," he says as he tries one of the keys.

"I'd still feel better if I took a look," I say.

"Of course," he mutters under his breath. "Ah, there it is."

Turning the knob, the door gives, and he pulls it toward him. Beyond it is darkness.

"As you can see, there's no electricity back here. As I said before, no one goes here. At one time, this was a ballroom used for conventions and parties and the like, but there was far too much for the owners to fix, and they elected to close it down until they wanted to deal with it. We replaced the door with one that locks firmly, and I assume they blocked even that with the plywood to discourage curious guests."

"There's no electricity on this side of the hotel?" I ask, stepping closer.

"That is correct."

"Then what is that light back there?"

Mr. Robinson stammers for a moment, his eyes following my

finger, pointing to the far end of the ballroom. Behind stacks of chairs, draped with sheets, there is a pinprick light glowing in the distance. I watch his head turn sideways, and his eyebrow wrinkles before he turns to me.

"I haven't the slightest idea," he admits.

"Then let's get one," I say, moving toward the door.

"Miss Griffin, I must object. I don't know what kind of equipment is in there or how dangerous the room could be."

"I'll take my chances," I say and brush by him. I step into the darkness, and my footsteps echo off the hardwood floors. I turn back toward him. "You coming?"

There is a moment's hesitation before he nods. "Yes," he says.

"And that's Agent Griffin to you," I add.

I pull out my phone and turn on the flashlight. It illuminates the room quite well, and I take in the vastness of the space. Tables and chairs are pushed against either wall, sheets draped over them gathering dust. I go up to a few of them, crisscrossing the room, looking for obvious signs of someone being here. Nothing jumps out at me, so we continue moving through.

"I just don't understand there being a light on," the manager wonders aloud as he stays rather close beside me. "The electricity in this part of the hotel has been off for some time. It has done wonders for the power usage. This room was extraordinarily difficult to heat in the winter and cool in the summer."

"I imagine," I note as I sweep the light up the walls to the high ceilings above.

I point the flashlight down toward where the tiny emergency light is shining. It does little to illuminate the giant room, but it does give me the impression that nothing will impede us, so we head that way. As we reach the end of the hall, the light hangs above us, and we both stare up at it. Just below it is another door. There is no lock on it.

"It's an industrial kitchen," he says without prompting. "When they would have weddings and things of that nature here, this is where all the cooking would be done. It's dark in there, so I assume the electricity has been off in there for a long time. The emergency light must have been given an exception for some reason."

"Or," I said, pushing the door open. As soon as I am inside the room, I reach for the wall. My fingers stumble across it until I feel the plastic underneath, and I flip the switches with one finger.

The room lights up in brilliant white light.

"This is ridiculous," Mr. Robinson says beside me. "These lights should be off. All of these lights should be off."

"Shh," I say, putting one finger to my lips and holding my other hand out to him. "Do you hear that?"

"Hear what?"

"The low humming sound." Somewhere on the edge of my hearing, a hum drones at the lowest pitch. It's constant yet quiet. Like an appliance that was left on.

"I don't.... oh, wait," he says, suddenly seeming to catch the sound.

"What is that?" I ask.

"Miss Griffin, I don't know. None of this is making any sense to me."

I follow the sound across the kitchen. The islands in the middle of the room are on wheels, but none of them seems to have been moved in some time, judging by the fine layer of dust on the floor. Except one. It is set beside a large metal door, and a streak of clean floor seems to suggest it was shoved there recently; the area around it has marks that look like footprints mixed together.

Suddenly, I realize the room is very cold.

"It's the freezer," I say, pointing to the metal door. "The freezer is on. And someone has been here not long ago." I walk up to it despite a blubbering objection and a hand that reaches out to stop me. When I yank the door open, the cold air washes over me, and the chill runs up my spine.

But the chill from the cold is nothing compared with the one I get when I look down. Just beyond the door, to see the lifeless, frozen body of Lydia Walsh.

. . .

"You saw her on the video. She was obviously extremely drunk, or high, or something," the manager stammers as soon as he sees the body. He doesn't even recoil or act surprised. Immediately, his lips just start moving in an attempt to blame the victim, the woman who once lived inside the skin lying near my feet. But his yammering is falling on deaf ears.

"You need to call the police right now. I'll need to take pictures for evidence," I say.

He doesn't budge at first, and I take another step toward him. When I do, his eyes, which had been locked on Lydia, move over to me. Finally, he nods and takes a few steps away from the freezer, pulling his phone out of his pocket. I watch him dial and notice his hands don't shake. His voice doesn't warble when they answer.

"Yes, I have to report a dead body," he starts, looking over his shoulder at me. I turn to take pictures but keep my ear out for him.

Poor Lydia. She's curled up in the fetal position, as if she was trying to stay warm in her final moments. I take dozens of pictures, getting as close as I can without touching her, moving to different angles. I see no visible wounds. She must have frozen to death.

"Some girl," Mr. Robinson's voice cuts through my thoughts, "got drunk or high and wandered down into a restricted area of our hotel."

He is laying the foundation for denying liability, shifting the blame to Lydia. But I know better than that. I might not have known her extremely well, but I knew she wasn't the type to get blitzed and lock herself in a freezer. Especially when she thought she was working on a case.

"A restricted area that somehow has electricity," I interject. Mr. Robinson sighs heavily. "Of course," he continues into the phone, "I can meet the officers outside and bring them right in. Thank you."

Pulling the phone away from his ear, Mr. Robinson stuffs it back into his pocket and stands there, his eyes falling back on the body. I turn toward him, and he looks back at me. I still can't completely read the expression on his face.

"Why did this area of the hotel have electricity if you said it was shut off?" I ask.

"I would like to know the same thing," he says, his hand sliding through his hair in exasperation. "But you saw the tape. You saw her tripping and stumbling and talking to people who weren't there. She was clearly on something, Miss Griffin."

"I don't know about that. Maybe a toxicology report can give us that information. But what I *do* know is that I see a dead body, locked in a freezer you say should not be working, on a floor, she should not have had access to, with electricity that should not be available. I need answers, Mr. Robinson. And I need them immediately."

His jaw opens and shuts a few times, and then he grasps the edge of the cart in front of him and bows his head. I am about to grill him again when a buzzing sound in my pocket stops me. I pull out my phone and grimace when I see the name flash across the screen.

"I have to take this. Why don't you go meet the officers outside? I will stay here until they get here," I say.

As he reluctantly walks away, I swipe the call button and turn away from Lydia's forever stare. I can't bear to see her like that, right now.

"Hi Millie, what's—" I begin.

"Emma, I need to speak to you right now. It's urgent."

Her voice is frantic, and I try to calm her immediately.

"Millie, calm down; I'm an hour away. What's going on? Are you okay?"

"I just need to speak to you. In person. Please, Emma."

The investigation team filters their way into the room, and I back up to let them through.

"Okay, Millie. I have something I have to wrap up here, but once I'm done, I'm on the road to you, alright?"

"Thank you, Emma. Meet me in the park. I have to go," she says, and then abruptly, she hangs up.

I look down at my phone in confusion and then up to one of the approaching officers.

"I understand you are FBI?" the man asks. I show my badge and give him my ID number, which he writes down diligently. I proceed to describe the evening to him and then give him my contact information before going back to Mr. Robinson.

"David," I say, keeping my voice low, "I have to leave now, but I am not done speaking with you. Something's wrong here, and I think you know more than you're telling me. I'll be in touch."

With that, I walk away, back out into the dark ballroom and through to the main hotel.

CHAPTER THIRTY-FIVE

I snap my phone into the holder on the dash and wait for it to connect to the Bluetooth. As soon as it does, I dial Sam's number and hit the gas. He answers on the second ring.

"Hey, babe," he starts. I hate to cut him off the way I am about to, but there's no time.

"I need you and Dean to meet me at the park. Millie called me frantic; she's really upset and wants to see me in person," I tell him.

"Oh. Um, sure. Alright, I'll head that way in just a few minutes. How far out are you?"

"I just left. I should be there in a little less than an hour."

"It's an hour away, where you are," he says, a disapproving tone in his voice.

"I said I will be there in a little less than an hour. Please, just meet me there."

Thankfully for both of us, he decides not to argue. I push the speed up and zip down the road. If someone pulls me over today, I am not above pulling the Bureau card and giving a traffic cop the scare of his career.

The trip is remarkably smooth, and I arrive in town within about forty-five minutes. My phone call to Dean is even more to the point than the one to Sam, but he will be bringing Xavier with him. When I get to the park, I pull into the large gravel parking area just off the road, and I find Sam's car. I park beside it, and before I can even exit, Dean pulls in beside me.

Sam walks over to me and kisses me on the cheek. "You didn't tell me what happened at the hotel," he frowns. "Everything okay?"

"It's a whole thing," I shrug, looking up to the entrance to the park. Xavier and Dean wait by the back of Dean's car, and when we reach them, we all walk together.

"I guess that's all I'm getting right now," Sam says.

"Once this is over with, I'll explain it all to you," I tell him. "I'm just worried about Millie."

As if on cue, from the entrance, Millie's head pops out. She sees us and begins striding toward us, nervously looking over her shoulder before breaking into a run. My instincts pick up, and I start to jog her way. I get a few steps before screeching tires and the growling sound of gravel being spit into the air turns my attention to a black sedan parked near the entrance.

The driver flings it in reverse and spins it to face directly at us. Millie is between us and the car, and she screams as it speeds toward her, its engine roaring angrily. Before she can dive out of the way, the car lunges at her, gaining speed quickly and overtaking her.

There is a sick crunch as the wheels roll over her body. I can do nothing but watch horrified as a tire drives her head into the gravel. I realize I am pulling out my gun as I dive out of the way of the oncoming car. Gunshots fill the air as both Sam, and I empty our clips into the car as it passes by, barely missing us.

The sedan peels out onto the street, trying to make a U-turn. It swerves wildly, and Dean chases after it. It only travels a block before it rolls off the side of the road, crashing into a telephone pole. Sam takes off toward the car, and I stand up, gingerly.

I look only momentarily at the mangled body of Millie, and then my heart breaks when I see Xavier curled up on the ground, just a few feet from her. His mouth is locked open, and his eyes are wide. One hand reaches out and touches her fingertips.

I'm torn about where to go. Sam has his gun drawn and is approaching the window of the car, and duty wins over emotion. I run toward Sam, tears stinging the sides of my eyes.

I change my clip, and I approach the passenger door while Sam goes to the driver's side. We each take measured, matching steps as we get closer to the front. If there is movement in the seat, we will both likely open fire, and we need to make sure we won't hit each other. As I creep up the side of the car, I notice that both tires have been shot out, one completely flat and the other missing entirely, the rim already dented by the road and the crash. Bullet holes dent the side of the car, and I wonder if I hit the driver.

I hope I didn't. I need the answers more than I need the vengeance.

I reach the passenger window and duck my head down to see inside. Glass is shattered all along the seat from the windshield. The driver had gotten an impressive amount of speed going for the short distance he made it on two wheels before crashing. I am noticing details about the crash, filing them away, noting that none of the bullets seem to have pierced the skin of his legs or arms before I catch Sam's expression.

His mouth is agape, and he is staring at the turned head of the driver. I can't see the face as it is turned away from me, but Sam's expression tells me he recognizes him. Rather than bother with asking, I run around the front of the car and to his side. What I see stops me dead in my tracks.

"Oh my god," I whisper.

Sitting in the driver's seat, his eyes glassy but lifeless, is Gabriel, from the grocery store. A small trickle of blood runs down the center of his face from broken glass, and the airbag is deployed to shove him back in his seat. A million questions run through my mind.

"Why is he dead?" Sam frowns, shaking me out of my own thoughts. "His airbag deployed, and we didn't hit him with the gunfire. How is he dead?"

"Almonds," comes a voice behind me, and I jump. Xavier closes the gap between us and peers inside. "I can smell almonds."

Sam looks over from him to me, a pleading expression on his face. I shrug and shake my head.

"What about almonds, Xavier?" I ask.

"I can smell them. Bitter. Bitter almonds. It's cyanide. This man killed himself."

I look back down into the lifeless face of Gabriel. Something seems to be stuck on his lip, and now that I have that idea in my mind, I know what to look for. I lean in closer and see it is, in fact, part of a pill.

"He's right," I announce, looking back to Sam and Dean. "He has a part of a pill still in his mouth. He must have chewed that pill when he realized he wasn't going to get out of here without being caught."

"But why?" Sam asks. "Gabriel? I just don't get it."

"What's that?" Dean asks, poking his head inside. "There is a necklace here. Do you see this, Emma?"

I lean back in and see a necklace hanging from Gabriel's body and pooling on the airbag. I take in a sharp breath when I see it.

"It's the key. The one that was stolen," I say. "What is going on?"

I take a step back; the world reeling around me. Nothing is making sense. And yet, everything seems to be falling into place. I try to turn away from the awful site of Gabriel's body, and my eyes cross over Millie again. A crowd is already forming at the edges of the park. I will have to get them to go away while we wait for the crime scene people.

Xavier walks back across the road, seeming not to notice the people who part for him. He goes back over to where Millie's body has fallen and lies back down where he was when I first noticed him. His hand goes back out and touches Millie's again. For a long time, I can't move. I am rooted to the spot, watching him look at her. It isn't until the sounds of sirens fill the air that I can get myself moving again. My soul hurts for Xavier and the way he is processing what he saw.

But I am also just completely confused. Before the investigators get to Gabriel's body, I walk back over to it. I can hear the cop approaching me, and Sam runs interference, just long enough for me to slip the necklace off him and shove it in my pocket. When I walk away, I notice I got a bit of his blood on my hand, and I instinctively wipe it off on my pants as I move on.

CHAPTER THIRTY-SIX

Time slides by. I've completely lost track of it.

I can't stop seeing Millie's face, the blood trickling down it and dropping onto Xavier's arms as he scooped her into them. She just lay there, pouring out her blood onto the ground, and there was nothing I could do. I stood there and watched her murdered right in front of me, and there wasn't a single thing I could do to stop it.

But it's another face that's hitting me even harder. Gabriel. So young and sweet. Full of life. Until the moment he put that cyanide pill in his mouth and smashed his car.

I just don't understand. I can't understand.

Why was he here? Why Gabriel? Why cyanide?

It's obvious his running over Millie was no accident. Just watching it was proof enough. There wasn't a single second of hesitation or slowing down. She was his target, and he mowed her down. But even if it hadn't been for watching how he hit her, the fact that he killed himself within moments tells so much. And yet, nothing. He never got a chance to speak.

And then there's Lydia. Brought out of one freezer only to be stretched across a slab and put into another. No one is taking either of the cases seriously. The investigation into Millie's death has been surface-level, barely existent. The police say it's an open-and-shut case. The solution is right there. It might not make any sense, but Gabriel ran over her, then killed himself out of guilt.

There's no reason to dig any deeper. It will only cause pain.

It's different for Lydia, and yet so much the same. The police said the right things. They searched around and took pictures. They watched the same surveillance I did. They searched through the same belongings now packed in the corner of my room because I don't know what else to do with them.

And all they can say is it had to have been an accident. Her body showed no signs of assault. She wasn't shot or stabbed. Her fingernails were pristine, which means she didn't claw at the door to the freezer or try to get out.

But that surveillance footage was suspicious. Not in that it showed she was murdered or what might have happened to her. Instead, it was suspicious purely because of her behavior. She seemed erratic, impaired. As soon as they saw that, the police framed the entire situation as a tragic accident, a woman who indulged too much and found herself trapped in a freezer where she passed out and froze.

Only, there's still no explanation as to why the freezer was even on. The manager admits that section of the hotel is completely off-limits. When the owners decided to stop offering services in that area, they wanted it disconnected from the rest of the hotel as much as possible. Turning off the electricity and water meant no heating or cooling bills. A huge savings.

Except that there was a freezer left on. Something like that is easy to overlook when you want to cast blame on the woman who died rather than find the real answer.

Both of these women are dead, and everyone is just pushing them aside.

I've been torturing myself over it. Even if I am their only voice, I will scream for them. These aren't women I particularly got along with all the time. I clashed repeatedly with them. Disagreed with them. But neither one of them deserved what happened to her. No one had the right to take their lives, especially the way that they did.

And if it's up to me to find out what happened to them, I will do whatever I need to. I am not the only person whose life these women walked through. And it's for those other people I will make sure neither is forgotten.

I will be Lydia's voice for Greg and for what he hoped for with her.

I will be Millie's voice for Xavier and what he once had and still carries inside him.

I have the TV on just to give me sound. It has faded into the background. I can't even tell what's on until I hear Lydia's name. I look at the screen and see a picture of her smiling out from above the shoulder of the dark-haired news anchor. She's reading out the story as if she doesn't even hear what she's saying. It's just words she's reading, without connecting them to each other.

She rehashes the story of Lydia's mysterious death, then shifts over to a recorded interview. Rachel Duprey's cold eyes stare at me.

"Over the last few days, many people have asked me how I feel about this hotel ending up in the news again," she says. "I'm here to tell you I am angry. I'm offended and upset. And I'm disappointed. It doesn't matter to me that the name of this hotel has been spoken on the news again. It doesn't matter to me that the image of the hotel is being seen all across the country. What matters to me is my father's name is still being linked to it. Ten years after his death, he is still being dragged into a salacious story that should never have been told. For so many years, I have wanted this all to be over and my father's good name to not only be restored but protected. I have taken such strides in that direction, but it is disheartening to see that so many people still want to hang onto what happened outside that hotel twenty years ago rather than know the truth."

"Can you confirm that the dead woman was at the hotel investigating your father?" an unseen reporter asks.

"I can't tell you why she was there," Rachel says. "I can confirm to you I spoke with her about Lindsey Granger on one occasion. It was a brief conversation because there is nothing more than brief information to offer. I told her the same thing I will tell anyone who asks about that dark incident in my family's lives. Nothing happened. My father was defamed and presented as two things he would never bear to be. A liar and an adulterer. There was no basis to those claims then, and there is no basis now. That's all I will say about the matter."

"So, she was at the hotel because of your father?" the reporter asks.

"I have said all that I will say," Rachel says. "If you'll excuse me, I need to get back to work."

I pick up the remote and rewind it so I can listen to the interview again. Something jumped out at me. Something that Rachel said isn't sitting well, but I'm not sure why. After listening again, I go over to Lydia's possessions and pull out her computer and all the notes she made. Digging through them, I start to piece something together.

A loud sound startles me out of my concentration. It happens again, and I realize something hit the door to my room. I open it and find Xavier with his back pressed against the wall, one hand over his eyes as he struggles to breathe.

"Xavier," I say. "What's wrong?"

He shakes his head, swallowing. His mouth moves like he's trying to say something, but no words come out. I try to take hold of his wrist, but he pulls away.

"No," he says. "Why me? Why am I here?"

"I don't know," I say. "You want to come into my room with me?"

"Not here, Emma. Here. Why am I here? There have been so many chances. So many possibilities."

"Come on inside, Xavier," I tell him softly.

His breaths are so shallow and fast; I'm afraid he's going to pass out. His skin is pale and sweat darkens the hair at his temples and makes it cling to his face.

"I want to take it off," he says, clutching at his arm, then at his chest.

"What?" I ask. "What do you want to take off?"

"My skin," he says. "I need to get out of it. I can't. I can't be in it anymore."

"Xavier, where's Dean?"

"I don't know," he says. "Help me, Emma. Help me take my skin off. I just can't. I can't do it."

"Yes, you can, Xavier. Come with me. Come into my room with me," I say.

"No," he says, shaking his head adamantly. "Three more days. Did you know that? Three more days?"

"Until what?" I ask.

"Three more days," he repeats. "I have to get it off. It's choking me."

The elevator door opens, and Dean rushes out. He looks relieved when he sees Xavier standing with me.

"I was taking a shower, and he left," Dean says.

"Help me get him inside," I say. "I think he's having a panic attack."

"Everything is right here," Xavier says. "Right here. Right on the tip of my tongue. Right on the edge of my mind. I can't figure it out. It's just not there. We have pieces of a puzzle, but not all of them. It's like putting together all of a person but not having the piece with their eyes. You can't see them. You don't know who they are. They're not all there."

"It's going to be all right," I tell him. "Do you need anything? Can I get you peanuts?"

"Nothing's going to be alright," he snaps, his voice ragged. "Nothing feels right anymore. No home. No comfort. No peace. Not until this is fixed. Nothing is right until this is fixed."

His head drops back against the wall, and suddenly he slides down until he's sitting on the carpet. It's as if every drop of energy just drained out of him, and he can't even support his own body anymore. Dean reaches down and helps him carefully to his feet.

"Bring him into my room," I instruct him. "It's closer."

I'm already on my way down the hall.

"Where are you going?" he asks.

"To find the pieces for him," I say.

CHAPTER THIRTY-SEVEN

Three days. I can't believe I forgot.

I didn't forget. I got so lost in myself. I didn't think about it. So tangled in finding the end to this spiral, I stopped paying attention.

Three days. October 21st. The anniversary of the day, Andrew Eagan died.

The day Xavier lost so much of his life as well.

He's not going to lose any more of it.

After he has been doing so much better, seeing him get so torn apart by his anxiety and agitation again cut deep. I hate seeing him that way. I hate watching his own mind torment him until he can't even bear to exist within himself.

His world is collapsing around him. The reminder of his best friend's death looming over him is made worse by having to face the courts again and pray they understand he was not the one who killed Andrew. To face all of that with the last moments of Millie's life fresh in his thoughts would be too much for anybody. I'm afraid it will destroy him.

I don't even bother trying to approach Lilith's house cautiously. I'm done with that. Whatever game she's playing, she's done.

I storm up onto her porch and pound on her door with my fist. I hear nothing inside the cabin. I pound again, but there's still no answer. No movement. The space inside the house is so small, if she was in there walking around, I would be able to hear her. The one time I come that it's deathly urgent, and she's not home.

I make my way back to my car in long, determined strides. I reach for the keys in my pocket, and my fingers tangle with something. Shaking my hand loose, I look down and see my earbuds on the ground at my feet, the rubber wire coiled around. I forgot I even stuffed them in my pocket. Scooping them up, I hold them in my palm and stare down at them.

I have them because they make hearing phone calls easier.

How can I not have thought of that? Getting in the car, I check my phone to see if I have any reception. Of course, I don't, so I race back to the hotel. Not even bothering to go inside, I sit in the parking lot and scroll through the various news articles and blogs about Lydia's death. Switching over to the videos tab, I find the clip of the surveillance video that was leaked to the media.

The piece of video went viral, with tens of thousands of people making mocking comments and making fun of Lydia for looking crazy. I have to admit; I harbor a little bit of hate for every single person who made one of those comments. They sit there watching the video, so easily making fun of her while forgetting they're watching a dead woman.

A dead woman talking to herself.

Just like Xavier thought.

I watch the video over and over, then look down at the buds still clamped in my hand.

She's on the phone. She's not imagining things, as they say she is. She's not crazy. Her phone is in her pocket, and she's talking through an earpiece. The phone was found in her room, but not the earpiece. I bet a more careful search of the hotel will uncover it.

But who was she talking to? Why was she acting so strangely? And why did she end up frozen to death in a freezer that wasn't even supposed to be on?

Whoever was responsible for getting her in that freezer put her phone back in her room. Either the killer didn't want people to know she had it with her, or he wanted it to look as if she just left everything and walked away.

———

I walk back into my room cautiously, not wanting to startle Xavier. But I find him lying on the bed, calm and almost subdued.

"Are you okay?" I ask, sitting at the edge of the bed.

"I slept for a little while," he tells me.

"That's good." I look at his face and see a dark strand of hair stretched across one eye. "Can I move your hair?"

He nods, and I brush it away gently.

"I'm sorry," he says.

"Xavier, you have no reason to be sorry," I say.

"We're here for you," Dean says. "For who you are."

He nods again. "I know. But I'm sorry for not telling you everything."

My stomach twists. I don't want to hear more.

"What do you need to tell us?" I ask.

"I fell in love with Millie a long time ago. We were friends at first. We were just children. Then, I began to see her differently. She was more. She was everything. But getting to know her meant getting to know her brothers. They were nothing like her, but they molded her to listen to them. As we got older, I noticed more and more how much they had a hold on her. They could control her so easily. "

"That's when you found out about The Order," I say.

"Yes," he nods. "It wasn't something that happened quickly. It took years. But when Andrew got to know them separately from me and they tried to bring him in, I started to learn more."

"He told you?" I ask.

"Some. Bits and pieces. Enough," he says. "And he died for it."

"They didn't choose him to kill because he told you about The

Order," I say. "There had to be another reason. If they thought you were a risk, they would have just killed both of you like Lakyn."

"I don't blame Millie for helping them," Xavier says. "She had no choice. I just hate that I can't prove any of it. I can't find that missing piece that would make it all fall together."

"What about Lilith Duprey?" I ask.

"What do you mean?" he asks.

"What does she have to do with The Order? She's a woman. There are no women in The Order. There never have been. Not in any of the chapters. So, why does she have so many connections to them? Could it have something to do with her husband? What do we know about his death?"

"No one was ever arrested for it," Xavier says. "Off in the wind. Random act of violence."

"So, it wasn't an initiation," I say. "If it was, someone would have been arrested and convicted."

"Right," he says. "But he was found in his bathroom. He wasn't disposed of somewhere. It doesn't fit the puzzle. A different puzzle, but not this one. He could have been linked to The Order. But he wasn't a part of the Harlan social circle or political sphere. All of that stayed in their original town. How would he be affiliated with the chapter here?"

"I talked to my father about that," I say. "He told me each of the chapters governs itself individually and operates independently of the rest. But they are still a part of the overarching Order of Prometheus. Which means, sometimes there is interaction between the chapters. Large events. Gatherings. It's possible he was a part of a different chapter that associated with the one here. Maybe after his death they worried about Lilith and wanted to make sure she was alright, so they decided to take care of her."

"Does that truly sound like The Order to you? Do wolves take care of sheep?" he asks.

"No," I admit. "And if even if there was going to be anyone taking care of her, I suppose it would make sense for it to be his chapter, rather than a different one, even if it was in her area."

"Yeah," Xavier says. "I don't think it's like a national museum exchange program."

"Speaking of Michael Duprey, I have to go back to the Garden View. Would you want to come with me?"

"Why are you going back there?" he asks.

"I need to test a theory," I tell him. "Do you want to come?"

"No," he says. "Thanks, but if it's all the same to you, I think I'll stay here and get some rest."

"Sure," I nod. "Rest well."

I look at Dean, and he follows me out into the hallway.

"I'll keep a close eye on him," he promises.

"Please do. He's getting more agitated the closer we get to the anniversary of Andrew's death, and he needs to feel safe right now."

"He needs to have someone prove he didn't do anything wrong and find out why Millie had to die," Dean says almost aggressively. "Emma, we've got to make this right."

"I'm doing everything I can," I say. "I promise."

CHAPTER THIRTY-EIGHT

FIVE DAYS AFTER DEATH...

She would never have wanted anyone to see her that way. Of course, no one ever would.

It was all done alone, hidden beneath fabric and dirt. Far from where she was supposed to be. Even farther from where they would believe she had gone.

Nearly a week has passed now.

It would be nothing but days tumbling by after this. They caught up quickly for the dead. And yet, went by so slowly.

Tears were being shed for her. But how many of them were real? And which ones were crying for themselves?

CHAPTER THIRTY-NINE

The police have long since left the hotel. They'll be back. They'll check in a few times just to keep up appearances, so it won't look as if they've just thrown Lydia away. Even though they have. But for now, I'm glad they're not here. It makes it easier for me to walk in and cross through the lobby without being noticed.

I don't want anybody with me while I'm doing this. I need to be able to see it myself. Not influenced by anyone or anything else but my own senses.

I take out my phone and record where I'm going. Trying to do it by memory, I follow the same path Lydia did, looking at the same things she did. I'm trying to get her perspective. Exactly what she was seeing. Just as importantly, I want to see where she wasn't seen. The footage doesn't show everything. There are sections of the hotel that aren't covered, places where she must have walked.

Not just the abandoned area where she was found, but other places she must have passed through without being detected. If she could do that, so could someone else. I walk along every hallway, every dip, and curve where she walked and turned and talked. When I've done all of that, I head down the hallway toward the abandoned section of the hotel.

I would expect there to be a new lock on the door, but instead, it's just blocked by caution tape.

There are no security cameras in this area. No one knows I'm here. And I move through the door quickly enough that no one finds out. The feeling is just as eerie down here as it was the first time. Shining the flashlight of my phone down the hallway, I take note of everything I see until I get to the kitchen.

It doesn't make sense that she would have just walked into a freezer without any kind of reaction. That she would have accidentally frozen herself rather than trying to fight her way out. Unless she was incapacitated when she went in, but then somebody would have had to have noticed her being carried. And there would have been some indication from the body: a wound, poison. Something.

I walk up to the freezer and examine the area around it. I'm just about to walk out of the kitchen when I notice something strange about the edge of the freezer. It's built into the wall, but the edge furthest from me seems to protrude by just a fraction of an inch. I push past several stacked chairs and an old dishwashing table to get to the other side of the freezer. When I do, I discover the built-in freezer isn't the only feature on the wall. A small alcove is built-in beside it. There's a door. And I can see right through the window to the parking lot outside.

My heart jumps. I can't believe I didn't notice this before. It was hidden behind everything shoved into the corner, but here it is. A door likely used years ago for deliveries and vendors. It would have been easy to come right through here and to the freezer and bypass the rest of the kitchen, along with the other areas of the hotel.

And easy to get right back out again.

I have a feeling. It's one of those unexplainable things, something you can't really define, but you know to follow it. Sam always says he sees that exact feeling on my face and instantly knows I have to do something. Right now, that feeling leads me to reach out and test the door.

It should be locked. This area of the hotel has been closed down for so many years; it should have been secured the last time the staff used it.

Of course, the last person who used it wasn't the hotel staff.

And that's why it opens now. It doesn't swing open smoothly. There's resistance. But I'm able to push it open and step right outside into the staff parking area. There's a small loading dock, where deliveries of groceries and catered food used to come for the elaborate events held just inside. Like the rest of this section of the hotel, the loading dock is sleeping. Nothing has happened here in so long.

Nothing but an earbud being crushed into the cement.

I want to reach down and pick it up. But I stop myself. Instead, I take a picture of it, send it to myself just to be sure, then look around more carefully. Walking backward across the lot, I scan the back wall of the building. I catch sight of the emergency exit at the end of the hallway. The door the hotel staff assumed Lydia walked through to escape her bill.

She walked through it. But it was to escape a lock. The staff and the police had the lingering question of how Lydia got through the locked door to the abandoned section of the hotel, to begin with. But she didn't. She walked out of the emergency door and came around here. Something happened to her right here. Enough to knock her earbud out and crush it.

Now the question isn't how she got down to the abandoned area, but why? And who was waiting for her at this door?

I take a few more pictures, then slip back into the hotel using the emergency exit rather than going back to the kitchen. I've nearly made it back through the lobby when I hear a voice that makes my skin crawl.

"What are you doing here?" Rachel Duprey asks me angrily.

"I don't think that's any concern of yours," I say.

She tosses her head and lets out a sarcastic laugh. "No concern of mine? You're slithering around here like that woman, trying to find more ways to make a lousy buck off my father's ruined reputation."

"I'm an FBI agent, not a tabloid reporter," I tell her. "I'm investigating the scene of a crime."

"What crime?" Rachel asks. "You're not talking about Lydia Walsh? She gets drunk and wanders off into an area of the hotel she's not supposed to be in, and somehow that's a crime? Who committed it? The bartender who served her?"

"She didn't get in that freezer by herself," I snap. "Just like Lindsey Granger didn't walk away from here by herself."

I shouldn't have said that part, but I couldn't resist.

"That's enough," Rachel snaps. "I'm done with this. I'm done with you and every other slimy person who delights in making my father seem like a bad man and continuing to degrade him even a decade after his death. I came here to warn the hotel not to sensationalize my father anymore. And I'm going to extend the same warning to you. Don't cross me again."

"You do realize a threat against a federal agent is against the law," I tell her thinly. "And unless you want to find yourself with a charge of obstruction of justice on top of that, I suggest you leave. Now."

She draws in a breath and rolls her shoulders back. Without another word, she spins around and stomps away on sensible nude-color heels that are far too loud against the polished floor of the lobby.

For the next two days, I wait. Eric is researching for me, trying to find anything he can about Lindsey Granger. I've asked him for one very specific phrase, and I hope he can come through. It would be a bit of a miracle, but I can always hope.

That hope is starting to slip away, just a touch on the third morning, right before my phone rings.

"Check your email," Eric says.

"You got it?" I ask.

"Got it," he says. "Turns out there were some conscientious police and FBI at the time. Or pack rats. Whichever way you want to look at it."

"I'm just going to go with, 'You are amazing!'" I tell him. "Thank you so much."

"See you for Thanksgiving?" he asks.

"Hopefully sooner than that," I say. "Tell Bellamy hi."

I open my email and pull up the old surveillance footage Eric was able to unearth. It's grainy, not a smooth, ongoing recording. But it's enough. I watch Lindsey Granger walk through the hotel, following almost the same path as Lydia the day she died, and as I did the other day. She is more fluid, more confident. She doesn't dip into the side hallways or talk to anybody. She walks through the hallways to the section of the hotel now abandoned but then alive with events and parties.

And was never seen again.

According to reports, there were some sightings of her in the years to come. The most prevalent information showed she had done exactly as Rachel told me. Left with her tail between her legs and started a new life. That became the accepted idea among those who had vilified Michael Duprey. And he went on to do big things.

After, of course, moving to a quiet little place in Salt Valley with his wife to get out of the limelight and enjoy a simpler life. Only to be struck down in a brutal, random act of violence that cut short his promising, glowing life.

I don't believe that for an instant.

CHAPTER FORTY

"Emma," Sam says, rushing into the room.

"Hey, babe," I smile, feeling more optimistic than I have in a while. "What are you doing here? I didn't think you were coming back until later."

I go to give him a kiss, but I see the look on his face and stop.

"What's wrong?"

"Have you talked to Dean?" he asks.

"No, what's wrong?"

The door opens, and Dean rushes in.

"Is he here?" Dean asks.

"Is who here?" I ask.

He looks frantic, on the edge of completely falling apart.

"Xavier," he says. "I can't find him."

"What do you mean you can't find him?"

"I can't find him," Dean repeats. "When I woke up this morning, he was there. Just like he always is. Then I went to have a phone call with one of my clients, and when I came back out, he was gone. I looked all over the house, in the garage, everywhere. He's not there. So, I thought I would come look here. I still have my room here, just in case, so I thought maybe he had come to just have some time to himself."

"He doesn't drive, Dean."

"I know," he says. "But he had to have gotten somewhere, somehow. Because he's not in either place. He's been really agitated the last couple of days. I've barely been able to understand anything he's been saying. I sat up with him most of the night the last two nights, just trying to keep him calm and make him feel better."

He paces back and forth for a few seconds. "What if something happened to him? What if they find him?"

"Nothing is going to happen to him," I say. "Because we're going to find him first. But we're going to have to split up to look for him. We need to get to him as fast as we can."

"Okay, for the record, I can't be blamed this time if something happens to you when we're split up," Dean comments. Sam cuts him a look.

"Where?" Sam asks. "Where should we look?"

"The nearest baseball field," I say. "He loves baseball. I know there aren't any games being played right now, but this is Xavier. Dean, you know him. Look where he would be comfortable. Somewhere that would make him happy."

Dean nods, and we head toward the door.

"Where are you going?" Dean asks.

"Andrew Eagan's grave," I say. "Today is the anniversary of his death. It's really been weighing on Xavier, and I think it finally got to him. Maybe he would want to go and pay his respects."

"Keep your phone on," Sam tells me. "Get in touch if anything happens."

"Both of you, too," I say, giving each of them a hug.

"Love you," Sam whispers.

"Love you."

We split up in the parking lot, and I get in my car. I'm pulling out as I research where Andrew is buried. As I type his name, my mind shifts. That's not where he is. Xavier is anxious and upset. He's angry and sad and agitated. He's not going to go to the cemetery. He's going to go somewhere that gives him peace.

I know exactly where he is.

I shut the car off and wait for a moment in silence, hoping I will hear something, anything to guide me. A gentle, cool breeze moves leaves through the distance, and they collect against the wooden walls blocking the entrance to the theme park. The gate, rusted green by time and weather and disuse, is cracked open. There seems to be no movement I can see inside, but that means nothing.

Pulling the gun out of my side holster, I flip the safety switch off, just in case, before re-holstering it and step out of the car. I shut the door hard, knowing that if someone was waiting for me, they heard me pull in anyway. At least this way, maybe Xavier heard me. I walk up to the gates and peer inside.

There is a long, empty path, looking almost like a road, with facades on either side. At the end of the path is the Ferris wheel, the seats all removed, so it is just a big empty circle in the sky. As the breeze blows, the wheel moves a little but does not spin.

The path forks around the wheel, leading deeper into the amusement park, and then splits off in various directions, all the side paths presumably returning at some point to funnel people back to the entrance. I take a few hesitant steps inside and feel the darkness of the park closing in around me. My eyes begin to adjust to the lack of light, and I can just make out the names on the buildings above empty stalls.

Some of the stalls were clearly games, with empty bottles or a basketball hoop still set up. Time and disuse have worn the paint away from the backboard and the sign telling customers how much a toss costs. I briefly imagine the park full of life. The laughter, the music, the children running around with their prizes. The smell of fried food, the whirring of the rides, the tangible excitement, and the anticipation of being on the roller coaster.

I shudder at the stark difference now and push on. I pass by a drink stand that's worn away to nothingness, the roof having caved in on itself and the paint of the soda company logo long worn away. I try to get some sense of where Xavier might have gone. The loneliness of the large, empty park starts to weigh on my shoulders, and I shake it off.

Dean and Sam are busy looking elsewhere, but someone needs to look here. Xavier said this is a place of peace. On a night when he desperately needs peace and comfort, this would be a home of both, even in decay. Xavier wouldn't see it as empty or lifeless or dead. He would see what it once was, the energy that once filled it having never really left at all. He would see himself and his friend, still here and in that way, just as they always were. I try to see it the way he would. Where would he go?

My instincts take me to the left of the wheel. Something about how most people go right makes me feel more as if he would go the other direction. Less traffic moving his way. The path leads around the wheel and then veers off through a tunnel, long overgrown with vines and shrubs. I take a deep breath and enter the tunnel, keeping my eyes on the dim light at the end.

It is suffocating inside. The plant life that grew up around the sides, circling the metal and mesh tunnel, closed off the passage of air. The exit is so overgrown, I'll have to climb through it. The air inside is heavy and musty, warmer than outside. I can just make out footprints in caked mud along one side, and figure they have to be Xavier's. Transients wouldn't come this far out.

I holster the gun and push hard against a branch to create an opening. As soon as I climb through the brush, I hear something shift to one side. The light is brighter than I expect, and suddenly it's directly in my eyes, blinding me. I can barely make out the skeleton of a roller-coaster in the distance when something crashes hard into my chest.

I hit the ground hard, and I roll to one side to try to get my feet under me. Before I can use the momentum to stand, another blow to my chest sends me reeling, and I hit the ground hard on my shoulder.

Whoever it is kicks me hard in the ribs, and I wrap my arm around his foot. He stumbles for a second, and I try to roll with his leg, taking him down. Instead, he drops his weight on the back of my neck, and I go limp. My fingers tingle as I groggily try to get to my knees. I hear a sound of effort, and another hard kick connects, heel first, in my temple.

Gravel and dirt fill my senses when I come to again. It could have only been seconds because he's not on top of me, but I realize I was out. I scramble onto my back, rolling backward to create space and reach for my hip. The gun is still there, and I yank it out of the holster. Blood flows from a cut on the side of my cheek, and a rivulet streams into my mouth. I taste iron and dead leaves. I spit as I get to one knee and look back at my attacker, who has ceased pummeling me for now.

Whoever it is wants me to get up. Which must mean he isn't afraid that I have a weapon. I put one hand up to block the light that is blinding me still. I can just make out a shadow against it.

"Don't move," I yell, aiming at the blurry black shadow. I sidestep to move out of the direct glare. As I do, color filters into focus, and the face of the person in front of me becomes clearer.

It's him.

"Isn't this familiar?" the Dragon sneers.

"How?" I stammer. Before he can answer, I pull the trigger. I don't care how. I want him dead.

But the gun doesn't fire. I click it a few more times, my stomach dropping. I can feel the air as my eyes open wide as I pull the trigger over and over again.

"Missing these?" Dragon grins, kicking at the ground. Bullets roll in all directions. I stare at them, uncomprehending.

"You were out for a minute there," he says in mocking concern. "I thought our reunion was already over, but then you moved. I couldn't have you shoot me, but," he says, taking a step closer, his breath creating a halo of steam above his head, "I did want you to pull the gun out. For old time's sake."

He smiles at me, and I feel my stomach flip. It's the same wide but thin smile he had when he committed murder in front of me. The smile of a man who doesn't just think, but *knows* everything is under his control. He has ultimate power.

Even though the gun has no bullets, I stand there, training it on him still. My mind is racing, trying to think of what to do next. No one knows where I am, and even if they did, they wouldn't have time to get to me. I have to do this on my own. I have no clue if anyone else is here or what he has planned. The best thing I can do is go on offense.

So I do.

I toss the gun at him, not necessarily trying to hit him, but to distract him. He takes the bait and ducks as one arm reaches out to try and bat it away. I pounce, diving at his knee, smashing my own into it from the side.

He cries out and crumples to the ground, and I wrap my arm around his throat, staying on his back. I try to maneuver for a choke-hold, but he spins, making me lose my grip. I roll away, but he is faster and not suffering from a likely second concussion in a short span of time. I try to wrap around him by the torso as he reaches me, but he rains down a fist that connects with my jaw, and I feel myself lose strength as if it's flooding out of my fingers.

I fight to shove him off, but he is already mounting me, throwing haymakers at the sides of my head. I reach up to triangle him, trying to trap one arm and his head and choke him out, but he connects with his elbow on my jaw, and my vision fades. I don't feel the pain of the next hit, but I can feel my head react to the momentum, snapping it to the side. My eyes flutter closed, and the back of my skull cracks against the pavement.

CHAPTER FORTY-ONE

The ground moves beneath me, but I know I'm not walking. I can feel the dirt and wet grass brush against the skin of my lower stomach as my shirt stretches. My other arm is tingling and is raised above me. It dawns on me that I am being dragged. I try to open my mouth, but the effort is too much. I fade again.

Again, my eyes open. The world is blurry around me, but I am no longer moving. I am face down on concrete. Blood pools under my nose, and as I exhale, a bubble forms in it. I watch it as it moves across the puddle and then pops. The throbbing in my skull is intense. I close my eyes for just a second to block out the light.

I open them again, and I am sitting. The grogginess is fading fast, and I feel the world rapidly coming back into focus. There are what looks like hundreds of chains in front of me, coming down from above. I turn my head to the side and see that one is beside me too. My feet aren't touching the ground. Where am I?

My head lolls to the other side, and the world spins with it. I clench my eyes shut, but no time passes when I open them again. I am fully awake but in tremendous pain.

And in mid-air.

Suddenly, everything slides into focus, and I see where I am: high above the ground, my legs dangling from the swing. I stop letting my legs kick out of instinct, forcing myself to calm down. My hands aren't tied, but that doesn't stop the fear clutching my throat. A metal bar stretches across my lap, holding me in the thin leather seat. It connects to the two chains on the front, and when my knee hits it, it moves up.

I look around wildly, and ice courses through my veins at what I see. A person is in a swing a few dozen seats away, directly across from me on the other side of the pole in the center. I recognize him despite his being slumped over, his head curled into his chest. A single, dried line of blood runs from his forehead down his nose.

Xavier is hurt, and there is no metal bar securing him to his seat.

"Don't I remember your saying you loved the swings, Emma?" Dragon shouts from far below me. "Or was it that you hated them?"

I look down to see him standing in a box just outside the metal bars of the ride's barrier. A control panel sits in front of him, and the wireframe that once held a canopy to cover the operator is now bare, so I can see straight down to him. His toothy grin is wider now, and the light bounces off it.

"Let him go," I shout down to him.

"Poor choice of words, Emma," Dragon replies and presses a button. Lights suddenly fill the ride, and I squint against them.

"Bring us back down, or I swear to God..." I begin.

"*What?* You swear what? What good are your promises anyway?" he screams, spittle falling from his lips and resting on his chin. He doesn't even wipe it away as he speaks. "What do you know about power?"

His other hand holds a phone, and he presses his thumb into the screen. When he does, lights flood the entire area of the park. I can see for dozens of yards beyond the swings.

"I know about power," Dragon continues. "Like electricity, it flows through me. It's funny. This old place was abandoned for a long, long time. Yet all I needed to do was make *one* phone call. Just one, and poof."

Another press on the screen of the phone, and the lights of the swings come on. Music begins to play, and in the distance, the wheel comes alive, spinning with no seats. A ride for no one but the breeze.

Across from me, I hear Xavier stir, and I snap my head over to him.

"Don't move, Xavier. Stay where you are. I am going to get you out of this," I call over. "Just don't move."

"Okay, Emma," he mutters weakly.

"Power, power, power," Dragon grumbles below me, and I turn back to him. "People fear me, Emma. They fear my power. Fear is better than respect, you know. Big shot agent you are, you know about respect. But respect means nothing. People can respect you and still disobey you. But fear? When people fear you, they do as they are told. And on the rare occasions when they do not..."

He lets his threat trail off. His hand floats to a switch, and he flips it as he stares up at me. I feel my body jerk, and the sound of the motor comes to life in the pole. The swings begin to move.

"Xavier, hold on to the chains," I shout back at my friend.

"I can't!" he calls. "My hands..."

I move my gaze to where his hands are clenched between his legs. They are tied with a thick rope. There seems to be another rope tied around his elbows as well, the other end running down below the swing.

"Oh, God."

"Sometimes," Dragon continues below, "you have to teach people to obey. Like a dog."

The swings turn and gain speed. Xavier starts to slide as the swings' movement pulls them up parallel with the ground. He looks back at me with eyes that have no fear, no worry. Just resignation. This is the world as it is, right now. Maybe for the rest of his life.

"Shut it down," I cry out to Dragon. "You don't have the power you think you do. You still owe The Order. They will collect. So will the FBI. You can't outrun everyone."

As I spin, I can hear the echo of his laughter encircling me. Xavier is slipping inch by inch, and my mind is racing to figure out how to stop his slide.

"The debt to The Order is paid!" Dragon screams. "And my power doesn't stop at the doors of the law, Emma. I have friends *everywhere*."

Xavier cries out from across from me, and I look over to him, a scream filling my own throat. His body tumbles out of the seat, and the rope that holds him around his arms slips up nearly to his shoulders. I see the way it is tied in a noose above his back. The way he is spinning on the swings, all it will take is for him to slip further and further down, and the noose will tighten around his neck.

"Xavier, don't panic!" I cry out. "Try to stay calm!"

His eyes are rolling around as if he is taking in everything one last time. His lips move as he mutters to himself. I can't make out the words, but it seems as if he is doing a math equation.

"Too bad about Xavier Renton," Dragon calls from below. "So distraught by his inevitable return to prison that he came to a place he used to spend time, found his favorite ride, and took his own life."

My eyes make contact with Xavier's, and I watch helplessly as he slips further, the rope now just barely on his shoulders.

I've failed. Xavier is going to die here, and then I am going to die here, and Sam and Dean won't ever know what truly happened to me. And my father will have lost me again, and everyone I love in my life will be heartbroken. But then—

A boom crackles through the air below.

Dragon cries out in agony.

I look down as the swings revolve and see Lilith Duprey standing just beyond where Dragon was, a gun in her hand, the barrel smoking. Dragon lies crumpled under the controls, most of his body out of view.

"Lilith!" I call out. "Stop the swings!"

She reaches forward and slams her hand on a red button in the center of the console. I hear the motor die away, and the swings slow down. Xavier's hands and feet are tied together, but he is reaching up, trying to grab the rope around his shoulders.

"I'm going to bring you down," Lilith calls, and I feel the jerk of the swings lowering. When they do, Xavier slips further, and he clutches at the rope just before it slides up around his neck.

CHAPTER FORTY-TWO

"Stop!" I scream. The swings cease to move, and I yank on the metal bar that holds me in the swing. It moves up the chains easily, and I grasp them just below it and hoist myself until I am standing in the leather seat.

"What are you doing?" Lilith cries from below.

"I don't really know," I tell her, releasing the chain with one hand for a moment to let the bar drop and then grabbing it again. I repeat the action with the other side, and the bar drops all the way down to the seat. I place one foot on it and steady myself.

Xavier is hanging all the way across from me, one hand between the rope and his neck, his feet curled up under him like a frog to give him the slack he needs to get his hand up there. He is sputtering and in obvious pain but is still mumbling and looking over at me.

"I'm coming, Xavier," I call out, judging the distance to the swing beside me. I don't need to go all the way around; I can just cut across, but it still requires moving from swing to swing, high in the air. And Xavier doesn't have much time. Whether his hand is between the rope and the front of his neck or not; it will cut off his circulation and then choke him to death.

I take a deep breath and let go of the chain with my left hand. As evenly as I can, I reach out to grab the swing closest to me. It bounces off my fingertips. I nearly fall and grasp hard with my right hand to hold myself up, cursing under my breath.

My feet push down into the swing, and I rock a little, and a thought dawns on me. I keep the rocking going, and in just a couple of movements, I am touching the swing next to me.

Reaching out, I grab it and pull it with me on the backswing. As soon as I rock back again, I take the leap, clamping hard and jumping from one swing to the next. Both hands hold onto the chain tightly as I get my feet into place. I made it.

Only a few dozen to go.

"Just hold on, Xavier," I call out, trying not to let panic fill my voice. He has only a minute or two left before the pressure will be too great. I can't take my time.

I swing to the next seat, and then the next. If I wasn't so petrified for Xavier and for my own safety, I would feel like Tarzan, going from tree to tree. As it is, all I can think about is what happens if I slip, or worse, if Xavier does.

I am two swings away from him when I can make out a few of the words he is saying for the first time. I half expected a prayer or some mantra to keep him focused. Instead, it sounds like numbers. Statistics.

"Seventy-two percent chance at twenty feet, roughly sixty-six at twenty-one feet," he's muttering.

I make my way to the swing beside him and wrap my legs around the chain as to not lose my grip. I wrap my hands around the rope and tug, but I can't lift him without leverage. The pull on the rope also tightened it around his neck, and Xavier gags below me.

"Untie me," he sputters, his eyes finding mine.

"You will fall, Xavier. It will kill you."

"Not from this height. Untie me. Seventy-two percent chance of survival. Untie me."

I look at the noose behind his neck. Even if I could reach it easily, it would take a few minutes to unravel it.

"I can't," I say. "But I have an idea."

I reach under my shirt to my bra, a special pocket on the side of one cup that hides a small but sharp switchblade. I pull it out. Xavier looks at it with awe.

"Sam insisted I carry more than one weapon," I tell him, trying to keep my voice conversational. Keeping Xavier and myself calm is the most important thing. One wrong move and we both go down without warning.

"You two love each other very much," Xavier says, his voice becoming labored now. He tries a smile, but it doesn't form.

I try to smile too. "We do," I say. "Are you sure about this?"

"Seventy-two percent sure," he says matter-of-factly. "Sixty-six if we are twenty-one feet up."

"I don't like this," I say, placing the blade on the rope, just under where it is tied to the chair.

"Neither does the rope," Xavier counters. The part of me overwhelmed with thousands of emotions at once wants to laugh, but I keep my focus.

I saw until I feel the rope start to give way. Xavier looks up at me, and a wry smile crosses his face. I see his mouth is stained with dried blood. He nods.

"It's about to go," I tell him.

"I'm ready," he says.

There is a snap, and Xavier tumbles down. He lands with a sickening thud, and I scream for Lilith to lower me. The ride jerks to life again, and I unravel my leg from the chain. The ride is still spinning as it lowers, and I keep my eyes trained on him as best I can. When I am almost to the ground, and the swing is rotated away from Xavier, another gunshot splits the air.

I jump off the swing and tear back towards Xavier. A small smear of blood is under his head, but when I reach him, he doesn't seem to be shot. His eyes are open, and he looks up at me, seemingly okay.

"That didn't feel good," he says, and I exhale. I realize that I hadn't breathed out since the shot rang through the air. "The best way to fall from that distance is on your side. People try to land on their backs and break their spine. Or their front and shatter their face. But on your side..."

"Lilith?" I call out, looking up from the still mumbling Xavier. I scan the area where she had been standing by the controls, but she is gone. "Lilith?" I stand, looking all around me.

"Ninety-four percent chance of a broken hip," Xavier continues.

"Xavier, I'll be right back," I say. He nods but continues his statistics. If that distracts him from the pain he's got to be in; I'll take it.

"Lilith?" I say as I reach the control box. No one is there. Lilith seems to have disappeared.

And so has the Dragon.

I run for as far as the adrenaline will take me. Pain and exhaustion soon slow me down, and I make my way back to the swings to check on Xavier.

He's still lying on the cement, rattling off statistics and soothing himself with reassurances about how young he is and the rate of bone healing. I didn't find Lilith or Dragon. I'm about to turn around and try to force my way through the park again when I hear sirens. They scream through the trees and echo around me. Moments later, I see the lights flashing.

There's no reason to scream out. They know where to come. Lilith must have called them. She didn't want to be around when they got here, but she wanted to make sure Xavier and I got the help we need. It only takes a few more seconds before I see the ambulance. Behind it are several police cars and a second ambulance.

The EMTs stream out of the first ambulance as soon as it stops and race toward me. I shake my head, holding up my hands.

"Not me," I tell him. "Don't check me first. Check on Xavier. He's over there under the ride."

They take their equipment and run over to him. It only takes a moment for them to call out for the gurney. I step back and watch them carefully slide him onto a transfer mat and bring him up onto the wheeled table.

As they go by, I make sure Xavier can see me.

"Are you going to be okay?" I ask.

"I'll be fine," he says. "I can do this."

"Touch him as little as possible," I tell the EMTs. "Tell him before you do anything. Turn the lights off."

"You're not my mother," Xavier jokes. I smile at him, and he returns it. "Thank you."

"I'll come to see you as soon as I can," I say. "I'll have them call Dean."

He doesn't have much of a reaction. The emergency responders have already injected him with a sedative so his body can relax. His eyes flutter closed, and I feel a squeeze of worry in my chest. I hate that he's going alone. And he's going to wake up in a bright, unfamiliar room and might not remember everything that happened. I can only hope Dean will be there.

Once Xavier is loaded into the ambulance and it has driven away, the team from the second bus comes toward me.

"Do you want to climb in by yourself?" one of them asks.

"No," I say. They start to move the gurney out, and I shake my head. "No, that's not necessary either. What I mean is I'm not going to the hospital."

"Ma'am, you really should be checked out. You look as if you've been through something pretty rough yourself," he says.

"You can check me over, but I'm not going to the hospital. I don't have time right now."

"What do you mean you don't have time right now?" he asks.

"Look me over," I say. "Then let me go."

It seems to take forever for them to check over each of my injuries and clean up the ones they think are the most egregious. I'm running purely on adrenaline and determination. I can't feel the deep cuts or the stitches that have been torn away from my arm. I will. There's going to come a time, probably soon, when it all hits me.

I can only hope I've done what I need to get done first.

When they've relented, I thank the EMTs and run for my car. If I get there fast enough, I might be able to get away before the police realize they should be debriefing me on what happened. I'm lucky enough that they're so focused on trying to find Dragon that I can drive away.

My destination isn't very far. I get to Lilith's house and park. The door to her house is standing open, and I walk up to it.

"Lilith?" I call. "Are you home?"

There's no response. I walk around to the back of the house. I don't see anything. A tug in my chest sets my feet running toward the cornfield. I break through the barrier of trees and see the dark outline of someone sitting in the finished grid. All the bones have been removed, so the officers are no longer on duty. She's alone.

"Lilith?" I call, walking carefully into the field. "Are you okay?"

I realize she's sitting right where Lakyn Monroe was found. My heart leaps into my throat when I see the knife in her hand. The tip presses into her wrist, bringing up a small bead of blood.

"What are you doing?" I ask.

"I watched her," she tells me. "I didn't want to. Every second of it was horrible. But I couldn't look away. I couldn't let her be alone. So, I watched her."

"You watched her do what?" I ask.

"Die," she says.

"You were here?"

"Of course, I was. I'm always here. People just don't see me. I couldn't move that night. They had changed me. I don't know if it was because they wanted me to watch, or for some other reason. They rarely tell me. But I didn't close my eyes. Even if she didn't realize I was there, I wanted her to have someone. Someone to be there for her last moments."

"You put the cage over her," I say.

She nods and makes a soft sound of acknowledgement. "She was too beautiful not to. I couldn't stand the thought of the birds and the animals getting to her. I knew somebody would be looking for her. Some of them, nobody ever did. Either they weren't missed, or there just wasn't a way to find them. But her, she was something special. I knew someone would find her. I wanted them to find as much of her as they possibly could. I visited her. As much as I could. While I took care of the corn, I took care of her."

"All this time, it's been you," I say.

She nods and digs the knife a little deeper.

"Stop," I say. "Don't do that."

"I can't do this anymore, Emma. I've been doing it far too long."

"Why?" I ask.

"I fell in love," she says. "I was already married. But our marriage wasn't a happy one. If you listen really closely and read between all the lines, you'll find the truth to what it was really like to be married to Michael Duprey. Some moments very special. When he wanted to, he could treat me wonderfully. And he had the means to do it. But he also had the means to do it for any other woman who caught his eye."

"The, he did have an affair," I say.

"So many more than just one," she laughs caustically. "I knew about all of them. I pretended I didn't. It was easier that way. But I knew. I knew every time he had found somebody else. I could follow the progression of their relationship based on my own. But he always managed to be discreet."

"Until Lindsey Granger," I say.

She makes a sad sound and nods. "Until her. The thing is, I think he really loved her. I don't know if he ever told her that. Or if she had any idea other than the ring he gave her. But I really do think she was important to him. I just didn't want to give up that life. It was his idea to move to Salt Valley and try again. He didn't end up trying very hard, and my heart found somewhere else to be."

"Who did you fall in love with?" I ask.

"Sterling Jennings," she says. "He was a friend of Michael's. He was strong and confident. He was funny and made me feel beautiful. The more I loved him, the harder it got to be with Michael. He hated that Lindsey left him, and he was cruel and distant. I let Sterling convince me the only way I could live my life was to be without Michael. That I needed to save myself. He would always choose Rachel. Spoiled, vicious child, just a touch too fixated on her father."

"You killed him," I say.

Tears stream silently down her face, and for the first time, I realize how pretty she is. Her face is etched by time and worry, but the delicate details of beauty are still there.

"I thought I was getting my freedom," she says. "But I was just buying my way into hell. Now, it can be done. It can be over."

"No, Lilith," I say as she turns the knife. "Don't do that."

"I've done too much, Emma. I've been here and seen far too much. I know the faces that belong to the bones in this cornfield. I know what has come up out of that tunnel beneath the temple. I can't do any of it anymore. And I can't let them have me. They know what I've done. They know I helped you. I can't let them have me."

"I can protect you," I say. "None of this is your fault. They manipulated and intimidated you."

"Emma, I just can't. Every day of the last ten years, I've lived with this. And a constant reminder of what brought me here. I could never escape it. It was right there, all the time. I shouldn't be here. I don't deserve to be here. They took everything out of me. Everything that ever was worth anything. I'm ready for this to be over. Thank you, Emma. Thank you for finding her. And for finding me."

In one swift motion, Lilith slits her wrist from the heel of her hand down nearly to her elbow. I gasp and lunge toward her. Yanking off my jacket, I tie it tight around forearm.

"You are worth more, Lilith. You are worth far more."

CHAPTER FORTY-THREE

Horror rushes up through me, but I don't let it take over. Lilith needs me right now.

The blood is gushing fast, and she is already sagging, her eyes rolling back in her head. I tighten my jacket around her arm even more and pull her up to her feet.

"Come on," I tell her. "We have to get back to my car. Come on. Come with me."

She's weak and barely conscious, but I get her to follow me. I can't leave her sitting alone in the cornfield. If I do, I'll come back, and she'll be gone. I keep my phone in my hand and check it every couple of steps as we make our way back toward her house. Finally, I see one little bar appear. I call 911 immediately.

"This is Agent Emma Griffin, in urgent need of an ambulance," I tell them before the dispatcher even has a chance to respond. I give her the address. "Hurry. Please."

When we get to my car, I open the trunk and pull out my first aid kit. It has a tourniquet inside, and I'm able to secure it into place around her thin upper arm. One arm stays tight around her, propping her up as we sit on the hood of my car.

"Stay awake," I say. "Stay awake, Lilith. Don't let them take you like this. Don't let them have you. If you leave like this, you are offering yourself over to them. Don't let them. They've had enough. They have taken enough from you. Stay with me."

I keep talking, rocking her gently back and forth so the movement will jostle her awake if she lets herself drift off. I don't know what I'm talking about. I don't even know if any of the words even go together or form coherent sentences. All that matters is that she hears my voice. She knows I'm here. She's not alone. I won't let her be.

It seems to take forever, but finally, the ambulance screams into her yard, and the team I sent away earlier rushes out.

"She slit her wrist," I tell them. "The cut goes nearly to her elbow. It's wrapped in a jacket, and I applied a tourniquet."

"Good job," one of the EMTs says. "We can take it from here."

As they are loading her into the back of the ambulance, Lilith reaches for my hand. I take hers and squeeze it.

"They'll take care of you. You're safe with them," I say. She nods but doesn't let go of my hand. "Can I ride with her?"

When they agree, I climb up with them and sit beside Lilith, gripping her hand as they fit an oxygen mask over her face and call ahead to the hospital to prepare a trauma team.

As soon as we get to the hospital, the doors fly open. They run her into the back so fast I barely catch a glimpse of her before she disappears behind the double doors. I walk slowly inside.

"Ma'am, are you all right? Do you need help?" a nurse asks, approaching me.

I look down at the blood covering me.

"No," I say. "It's not my blood. Thank you."

Sitting in the waiting room, I call Dean and Sam. Tears are streaming down my face as I talk to Sam.

"I'm coming to get you," Sam says. "Just wait right where you are. I'll be there as soon as I possibly can."

Time is glacial. Half of me waits for any word about Lilith. Half of me waits for Sam. The clock ticks. At some point, I manage to clear my head enough from the shock to go to the restroom and wash off some of the blood from my face and hands. I return to my chair, the dull throb of pain in my shoulder growing louder and louder with every second.

Finally, the doors open, and he runs inside. I want to jump into his arms, but I don't have it in me. I don't need to. He drops to his knees in front of me and gathers me against him.

"I'm going to take you back to the hotel," he says.

"I have to be here for Lilith," I say.

"Emma, you need to get home now. I'll let them know to get in touch with you as soon as they know anything about her," he says. "You need to rest."

"Before we go, there's somewhere I need to stop," I say.

"Emma..."

"Sam, I need to do this."

Sam frowns but nods. I can tell it's breaking his heart to see me like this, to go along with this, but he does it anyway because he loves me. And I love him.

"Where do you need to go?" he asks.

"To the precinct. I need them to know I have a name for the body wrapped in the sheet in the cornfield," I say. "It's Lindsey Granger."

"Are you sure?" he asks.

I nod. "Lilith told me she could never escape the reminder of what she did. But it was right there all the time. That's because her husband did have a mistress, and she was buried right by the cornfield, where she was forced to work every day."

"She killed Lindsey Granger?"

"No," I say. "I'll explain everything to you. But I need crime scene pictures. I need pictures of the skeleton."

There's no way I can get out tonight. The only thing ahead of me is a long shower, and as much sleep as my body will give me. I know it's not going to be deep or restful. I'll be waiting every second for a phone call from the hospital. Dean is by Xavier's side, but Lilith is alone. I want her to know she hasn't been abandoned again.

The next morning, I wake up with every inch of my body in pain. My head throbs and swims. My mouth and throat feel sticky, as if I haven't had anything to drink in months. But I still pull myself out of bed. I have to. This has waited long enough.

Taking the pictures Sam brought me, I start the long drive. Sam knows where I'm going. I don't look in the rearview mirror, but somehow, I know he's there. Maybe somewhere in the distance. But he's there.

When I get to Rachel Duprey's office, I walk up to her receptionist and ask to see her.

"She doesn't wish to speak with you," the receptionist says.

"Try again, please," I say. "Tell her I need to speak with her about Lindsey's sheet."

With a confused look on her face, the receptionist picks up the phone and calls into Rachel's office. Seconds later, the door opens, and Rachel storms out. Gone are the measured, hyper-controlled strides. They've been replaced by heavy stomps, and the glare contorting her face is a far cry from the smile she paints on for every good cause and special event.

"I warned you," she says. "I gave you ample opportunity to act like a decent human being and not put yourself in legal trouble."

"I suggest you stop there," I interrupt. "Before you say something you won't want to be brought up in your trial."

Her eyes flicker over to the receptionist and back to me. She shifts uncomfortably.

"I don't know what you're talking about," she says.

"You got my message. I think you understand it," I say. "And if you don't. I have pictures here I would be more than happy to show everyone in the office. Unless, that is, you'd like to have a private conversation."

She looks at her receptionist. "Mary, take the rest of the afternoon off."

"Are you sure?" she asks. "If you don't want to be alone…"

"I'll be fine," she says. "Please let the others know as well."

The receptionist gets up to leave. I keep my eyes locked on Rachel. When everybody else in the office is finally gone, Rachel gestures me through her door. I step inside into her suit and take the folder out of my bag.

"You know, I really wanted to believe you," I start. "I really wanted to think you could be the good person everybody else thinks you are."

"I am that person," Rachel says.

I let out a short, merciless laugh. "I don't know whether you're just trying to convince everyone around you, or whether you actually believe it. But even you can't completely let go of it. You think you have. You think you've done enough good in this world to cover it up. But even you are still carrying it in your heart."

"What are you talking about?" Rachel asks.

"When you were doing the news interview, you said your father shouldn't be held responsible for something that happened *outside* that hotel twenty years ago," I say.

"Yes," Rachel says. "He shouldn't. He didn't have anything to do with Lindsey Granger and whatever happened to her. Neither of us did."

"Then how did you know something happened to her outside of the hotel?"

CHAPTER FORTY-FOUR

"Everybody knows Lindsey Granger walked out of that hotel," Rachel says.

Her voice shakes slightly.

"But you know why," I say, drawing one of the pictures out of the folder and showing it to her. "Tell me, Rachel, what did you say to her? How did you get her to meet you outside? Did you think your father was going to be there?"

She stares at the picture, her mouth trembling as she tries to find the next lie. In an instant, her eyes change. Something in her mind releases, and she's not trying to hide anymore. Words she has wanted to say for years bubble up inside her, and she has to release them.

"Yes," she says. "I told her my father was waiting for her."

"He loved her, Rachel. Did you know that?"

"No, he didn't," she snaps. "He didn't love her."

"Yes, he did. Even Lilith knows that," I insist. "If you had really wanted your father to be happy, you would have let him be with her. But instead, this is what you did to her."

I take more of the pictures out of the folder and toss them onto the desk in front of her. She reaches out and touches the pictures, her fingertips soft on their edges. She looks as if she's in a daze, not sure if she's actually here or not.

"I couldn't let her ruin him," Rachel says. "He had an affair. Men do that. All the time. But it can destroy the reputation and career of a politician. Especially one who is just getting started. I knew my father would do great things. From the time I was a little girl, I knew he would be one of the most powerful men alive."

"And how many times in your life have you said that?" I asked. "How many times have you said those words? Because you've now told me twice. Is it the narrative that you give everybody else, or the one you give yourself?"

"I had to fix it," she says. "He couldn't help it. Lindsey Granger seduced him. I had to make sure everything was okay again. I needed to make her go away. But I didn't intend to hurt her."

"Is this what you call not hurting her?" I ask, pointing at the pictures.

"It was an accident," she says. "I never intended to kill her. I wanted to offer her money. That's what I figured she wanted, anyway. I didn't think anything mattered to her but prestige and wealth. If I could give her enough money to set herself up with a good new life, she wouldn't need to keep interfering with my father. But she said no. She said she loved him."

"So, why didn't you believe her?"

"I thought she was just holding out for more. She knew she could cause a divorce between him and Lilith, which would be detrimental to how the public saw him. Nobody would trust him after watching him go through an extremely public divorce based on adultery. She was using it for leverage."

"Or, she was telling the truth," I reply. "She really did love him. Is that why she wore that ring?"

I point at the old ring found among the bones.

"I offered her a lump sum, then payments every year. She refused it. She was walking away from me. She was going to go call my father. I had to stop her. Just so that I could talk to her more. I reached out to grab her, but she moved away from me. There was a party that night, and a delivery truck was sitting right outside the door to the freezer. It was full of linens. When she turned, she slipped, and her head hit the back of the truck. When she landed on the pavement, I didn't know she was dead. I thought it had just knocked her out."

"What did you do? Did you call for help?"

"No," she says. "I panicked. If I called for help, everything would have come out. I had already come this far. I needed to keep going. The sheet was still warm from the laundry. They must have just washed it before putting it in the delivery truck. I wrapped her in it and put her in the trunk of my car. My father had a fundraiser that night, just as I told you. I had to make an appearance."

"You went to a fundraiser with the body of the woman your father loved stuffed in your trunk?" I ask.

Rachel runs her hand down the front of her throat as if she's holding back bile.

"After I greeted a few people and saw my father, I had to take care of her. The only place I could think of was the cornfield."

"Why?" I ask. "Was your father in The Order of Prometheus?"

"Yes," she says. "He became close with some members of the chapter in Harlan. He let me ride with him once when he came to meet with them in the cornfield. He told me they had business to handle."

"A body to get rid of," I remark.

She nods again. She must think if she doesn't say it out loud, it's not true.

"He didn't know that I knew. He thought I didn't see anything. He didn't know I followed him back three more times."

"You knew your father helped dispose of people, and you still thought he was a good man?" I ask.

"Yes," she says. "He was. He was a good man. And I was going to make sure he stayed that way. I got rid of Lindsey so he could be a good husband, even if I can't stand Lilith. I devoted my life to building him up and creating his career. I atoned for what I did. I fixed it."

"And Lydia Walsh?" I ask.

She shakes her head, closing her eyes and resting her fingertips over them for a moment.

"She just wouldn't stop. Neither of you would. She kept digging and digging. She was getting far too close to figuring it out. She might have already. So, I invited her to come to the hotel and get an exclusive with me. From spending so much time in the hotel when I was younger, I know more about it than the people who work there now, including where to find the circuit breaker. A fling with a maintenance man gave me that information."

She giggles, and I stare at her incredulously. "It's good enough for you, but not for your father?"

Her smile drops. "A fling. Three months and that was it. He could never be anything more, and both of us knew it. But he proved useful, didn't he?"

"I'm sure he would be thrilled to know he helped you freeze someone to death."

"Don't worry about her too much," Rachel says. "The drugs would have made her pass out well before the cold got her. It was a comfortable, easy death."

"Why did you drug her?" I ask.

"To make her more cooperative and easier to control. I needed to get her to follow my instructions and be caught on the security camera looking impaired. Then I led her out of the hotel and onto the loading dock. From there, I showed her the door to the kitchen and slipped her into the freezer. At that point, she was barely able to stand. She likely fell asleep in seconds."

"Don't try to sound compassionate. You built a life around lies and murder. Did you create the sightings of Lindsey Granger, too?"

"Yes," she says. "I couldn't let my father get hurt. Lindsey was an accident. Then when Lydia came, I couldn't let his legacy be ruined. It was just one more. And if you had just left well enough alone, that would have been it. But you couldn't. I won't let you hurt my father."

"He was a wife-beater and a philanderer," I say. "And if not a murderer himself, an accomplice to murder."

"Don't say that," she growls, her eyes wide.

"They know who Lindsey is now," I say. "They'll find her family and do a DNA test."

She shakes her head. "No. You. You caused this. If you're gone, it will all be gone. I won't let you hurt him."

She dives at me, her hands stretching for my neck. I try to reach behind me to grab my gun, but she is too fast, and I abandon that idea. Our arms tangle, and she pushes me into the wall, where we crash, pictures falling and shattering glass around us.

I feel my head pulled back as she yanks on my hair. As I slam my hip into her stomach, the wind escapes her lips, and she loosens her grip. I grasp her shoulders and sweep her leg, forcing her down. As we land, her head bounces up, and I slip, smashing down into it. Her forehead catches me on the bridge of the nose, and an explosion of pain rifles through my face. Blood flows like a faucet, and I know it is broken.

The momentary distraction gives her a moment to scoot away from me. She kicks, her heel digging hard into my hip. She kicks rapid-fire into my side with both feet, and I curl up to block them. The broken nose makes my eyes water, and I rub my forearm across them to wipe them. When I look back at her, the kicking stops, and she scrambles to her knees, moving away from me.

I get to my feet quickly and grab her around the waist from behind. Popping my hips forward, I lift her and bring her flying backward, landing on her shoulders. The crunch of her body couples with the destruction of the room. A chair gets knocked over, and more things fall off the wall. Glass cuts into my cheek as I roll over onto my stomach. It digs into my hands, and it feels as if it's my lungs, a powder of shrapnel, making it harder to breathe.

My wounds slow me down, and I am not up as fast as I want to be, dragging my body to respond. We reach our feet around the same time, and I lunge forward, swinging a fist at her. She ducks and tackles me around the waist, shoving me back. We crumple together on the ground.

She doesn't move fast enough, and I slam my elbow down onto the side of her head. She cries out in pain, and I do it again. One hand reaches up to claw at my face, and I feel the adrenaline rush of my training kicking in. She is in the perfect position, and I have a split second to react.

I kick my legs up, wrapping the arm between them. I push down on my heels to get me up for just a second, and then a fall back hard, pulling her arm with me. I can hear the shoulder snap as I land and know I either dislocated it or broke it. This would be where she falls apart into a crying mess, and I can keep her docile until help arrives.

Twisting the grip I now have on her wrist, I wrench the shoulder even further, and she screams. I tighten my legs around her, then pick up one foot and slam it down on her chin. The resistance in her arm lessens. I do it again, and it all but stops.

"Are you done?" I call out to her, but she doesn't respond. I wrench on her wrist again, applying more torque to the shoulder, but she doesn't cry out again. She must be unconscious.

I shove her hand away and spin to a sitting position. I have only let her go for a second and am reaching out to grab her hand again when she suddenly turns toward me, and points my gun at me. I barely have time to fall backward as a shot rings out. I am on my back as the hand with the gun follows me, and I kick at it. The grip loosens, the gun falling to the ground beside me. I roll toward it, gathering it up in my hand and turn on my side to face the fleeing Rachel as she makes her way to the door.

I pull the trigger.

She slumps against the wall, crying out again, her fingers slipping off the door handle. At the last second, I had pulled the gun down from aiming center mass and shoot at her leg instead. She crumples, a silent scream stuck in her throat as she holds her thigh with the only arm that still works. Blood seeps through her clothes and around her fingers as she slides further down onto the ground, writhing in pain.

I sit up and realize my left arm didn't move with the rest of my body. I look down at it and see blood pouring out of a bullet hole, directly in the center of the still-healing gash from the scythe.

"Are you freaking kidding me?" I cry out at the arm that now suddenly overwhelms me with pain. I glance back over at Rachel, her face a mask of tears and bruises. I point the gun back at her and scoot back, so I rest against the far wall to wait. Before long, Sam will get here with backup. Until then, I sit, gun trained.

The sound of the door splintering under Sam's boot is one of the greatest things I have ever heard. It cuts through the pain and reminds me I'm still here. A team rushes in and surrounds us, but I won't back down.

"Emma," Sam says from beside me, resting one hand on my back and the other on my gun. He gently eases it down. "Come with me." He lifts me up into his arms, and I hear him talking into his radio. "I need a bus. Officer down. Agent Griffin has been shot."

He looks down at me and pulls me close to his chest. My blood seeps into his shirt, but he only presses closer.

"Sam," I murmur.

"I'm here," he says. "You're right here with me."

I hear Xavier's voice in the back of my mind. *You are where you are. She doesn't want to tie her soul here.* In that moment, I know the place, the surroundings, that matter to me the most is Sam. And he is where I want to tie my soul.

"Sam," I murmur again. He looks down into my eyes. He's fading, but I hang on long enough to say the words. "Marry me."

EPILOGUE

FOUR DAYS LATER ...

"Why do you get to leave your room?" Xavier asks. "They won't let me."

"That's because you can't get out of your bed," I say. "It's a lot easier to move around after getting shot through the arm than it is after breaking your hip and two ribs and separating your shoulder."

"They could put me on one of those table things. Strap me to it and then stand me up and wheel me around," he argues.

"Like Frankenstein?" Dean asks.

"Frankenstein's monster," Xavier corrects him. "Though, I suppose Dr. Frankenstein could have tested it. Or just ridden around on it for fun."

"If you find one of those, get me a matching one," I say. "This wheelchair still hurts all my bruises."

"The metal head strap stabilizing the upper half of your body probably wouldn't feel much better," Xavier points out. "But I'll see what I can do."

"You have got to stop disappearing from your room," Sam says, coming in and dropping a kiss to the top of my head.

"I didn't disappear. I came to see Xavier."

"How did it go?" Dean asks.

Sam nods and sits down on the chair beside Xavier's bed. It positions him near both of us, and I reach over to hold his hand.

"It went well. Rachel is facing enough charges to make the judge yawn when she was reading them out. Lindsey Granger's family was there. They wanted me to thank you, Emma. For finally bringing Lindsey home."

"I didn't find her," I say. "It wasn't just me."

"You're the one who realized it was her. If it wasn't for that, it might have been years before her body was identified. Because of you, they're going to be able to have a funeral for her this weekend and bury her next to her grandmother."

"I'm glad," I say. "How about Lilith?"

"Better. She's in the secure hospital ward of the psychiatric facility. She'll stay there until she's strong enough for treatment. It's going to take a lot of time, and she'll still face charges, but she's going to be able to make something of her life."

"Are you leaving Harlan when you're discharged?" Xavier asks.

"Not permanently," I say. "This isn't over. We still have a long way to go. A lot to prove. Sterling is still out there. The Dragon is still out there. He paid his debt to the judge with Millie's death, but he's not done yet."

"How do you know?" Sam asks.

"Because he's not the one who paid. Gabriel is. But why? What did Gabriel owe?"

THE END

Dear reader,

I hope you're enjoying Season 2 of Emma Griffin.

I am able to keep writing these novels, because of you!

I know the world is a bit mad and we're all just trying to get through the year.

I really hope that I was able to take your mind out of the chaos and give you a moment of peace.

I would massively appreciate if you could take a moment of your day to write a review for this novel.

Your reviews give me the motivation to keep this series going, and it helps me massively as an indie author.

The review doesn't have to be long, but however short or long you want.

Just a few seconds of your time is all that is needed.

When you leave me a review, know that I am eternally grateful to YOU.

My promise to you has always been to do my best to bring you thrilling adventures.

I hope I have fulfilled that. I look forward to you reading my next novel!

Yours,

A.J. Rivers

ALSO BY A.J. RIVERS

Emma Griffin FBI Mysteries

Season One

Book One - The Girl in Cabin 13*

Book Two - The Girl Who Vanished*

Book Three - The Girl in the Manor

Book Four - The Girl Next Door

Book Five - The Girl and the Deadly Express

Book Six - The Girl and the Hunt

Book Seven - The Girl and the Deadly End

Season Two

Book Eight - The Girl in Dangerous Waters

Book Nine - The Girl and Secret Society

Book Ten - The Girl and the Field of Bones

Other Standalone Novels

Gone Woman

Titles are now available on Audible. Type https://www.audible.com/author/ AJ-Rivers/B0833HF2GL in your web browser to browse Audible now. Not an Audible subscriber, type https://www.audible.com/pd/B08FXNYXFD *try a free month today.*